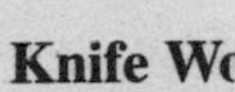

Knife Wo

Longarm threw his arm d hard into the padded wooden strips that formed Longarm's splint.

She cursed in frustration and tried to wrench the knife away.

Longarm twisted his arm, snapping the tip off the blade but freeing the knife for a slashing cut.

He pushed her away with his left hand . . . Janie recovered her balance, and came at him again.

Longarm was damn sure awake by then, adrenaline shooting through him like a charge of electricity.

"Hold it!" he snapped, reaching under his pillow.

For a moment Janie did halt in the middle of her assault.

"I don't wanta shoot you," Longarm warned, "but I will if I got to."

Janie's face twisted with hatred. "You're bluffing, you bastard."

"I'm telling you—"

She lunged for him again, the knife upraised ready to slash him.

He had no choice, dammit.

DON'T MISS THESE ALL-ACTION WESTERN SERIES FROM THE BERKLEY PUBLISHING GROUP

THE GUNSMITH by J. R. Roberts

Clint Adams was a legend among lawmen, outlaws, and ladies. They called him . . . the Gunsmith.

LONGARM by Tabor Evans

The popular long-running series about Deputy U.S. Marshal Custis Long—his life, his loves, his fight for justice.

SLOCUM by Jake Logan

Today's longest-running action Western. John Slocum rides a deadly trail of hot blood and cold steel.

BUSHWHACKERS by B. J. Lanagan

An action-packed series by the creators of Longarm! The rousing adventures of the most brutal gang of cutthroats ever assembled—Quantrill's Raiders.

DIAMONDBACK by Guy Brewer

Dex Yancey is Diamondback, a Southern gentleman turned con man when his brother cheats him out of the family fortune. Ladies love him. Gamblers hate him. But nobody pulls one over on Dex . . .

WILDGUN by Jack Hanson

The blazing adventures of mountain man Will Barlow—from the creators of Longarm!

TEXAS TRACKER by Tom Calhoun

J. T. Law: the most relentless—and dangerous—manhunter in all Texas. Where sheriffs and posses fail, he's the best man to bring in the most vicious outlaws—for a price.

TABOR EVANS

LONGARM

AND THE CROOKED MADAM

JOVE BOOKS, NEW YORK

THE BERKLEY PUBLISHING GROUP
Published by the Penguin Group
Penguin Group (USA) Inc.
375 Hudson Street, New York, New York 10014, USA
Penguin Group (Canada), 90 Eglinton Avenue East, Suite 700, Toronto, Ontario M4P 2Y3, Canada
(a division of Pearson Penguin Canada Inc.)
Penguin Books Ltd., 80 Strand, London WC2R 0RL, England
Penguin Group Ireland, 25 St. Stephen's Green, Dublin 2, Ireland (a division of Penguin Books Ltd.)
Penguin Group (Australia), 250 Camberwell Road, Camberwell, Victoria 3124, Australia
(a division of Pearson Australia Group Pty. Ltd.)
Penguin Books India Pvt. Ltd., 11 Community Centre, Panchsheel Park, New Delhi—110 017, India
Penguin Group (NZ), 67 Apollo Drive, Rosedale, North Shore 0632, New Zealand
(a division of Pearson New Zealand Ltd.)
Penguin Books (South Africa) (Pty.) Ltd., 24 Sturdee Avenue, Rosebank, Johannesburg 2196,
South Africa

Penguin Books Ltd., Registered Offices: 80 Strand, London WC2R 0RL, England

LONGARM AND THE CROOKED MADAM

A Jove Book / published by arrangement with the author

PRINTING HISTORY
Jove edition / January 2009

Cover illustration by Miro Sinovcic.

For information, address: The Berkley Publishing Group,
a division of Penguin Group (USA) Inc.,
375 Hudson Street, New York, New York 10014.

ISBN: 978-0-515-14572-4

JOVE®
Jove Books are published by The Berkley Publishing Group,
a division of Penguin Group (USA) Inc.,
375 Hudson Street, New York, New York 10014.
JOVE® is a registered trademark of Penguin Group (USA) Inc.
The "J" design is a trademark of Penguin Group (USA) Inc.

PRINTED IN THE UNITED STATES OF AMERICA

10 9 8 7 6 5 4 3 2 1

Chapter 1

Longarm sat slumped in a wicker rocking chair on his landlady's front porch. He was filthy dirty, unshaven and hungover. The voice of the newsboy on the corner hounded him.

"Deputy marshal guilty of manslaughter! Read all about it. Read all about it!"

The inquest had been . . . He tried to think. Two days ago? Three? He honestly could not remember. Wait. It must have been yesterday for it to be in the newspaper today.

He remembered the verdict well enough, though. Manslaughter. Guilty as sin. Gunned down his own good friend, Denver police lieutenant Ezra Jameson.

Oh, it was accidental. Of course it was. If the coroner had not believed that, they would have brought back a charge of murder.

An accident. But even so . . .

Longarm had been responding to a tip that the Curlew & Jones Bank was being robbed. How the fuck was he supposed to know that Ez had been tipped off as well?

He saw movement in the shadows. Saw starlight reflecting on a gun barrel. He fired.

It was as simple as that.

It was as terrible as that.

When men came with lanterns, they found Ez lying there with Longarm's bullet in him. Willing hands carried Ezra to Dr. Faber's office, but it was no use. Ez died sometime before dawn that same shitty night.

Custis Long had not drawn a completely sober breath since then.

Come to think of it, he did not really intend to. Not for quite some time to come, thank you very much. Right now life was entirely too shitty to be looked at without a gauze of rye whiskey to peer through.

"Deputy U.S. marshal guilty of manslaughter! Read all about it!"

Longarm wished the little bastard would shut the hell up. He wished his head would stop pounding too. He wished . . . he wished a whole heap of things, none of which was very likely to happen.

"Sir. Sir! Are you Marshal Long, sir?" He felt a light tug on his shirtsleeve—he had no idea where he might have left his coat—and opened one eye. "Sir?"

A boy of twelve or maybe fourteen was standing there. The kid was carrying a large pouch.

"What's the matter with you? It's bad enough you shout the news to every-damn-body. Now you have t' come up here on this porch an' rub my nose in it? Is that what you want?"

"I don't know what you mean, sir. I'm just a messenger."

"You're not . . . Never mind. Whadaya want with me then?"

"I have a message for you, sir. From United States Marshal Vail's office."

Longarm rubbed his eyes and tried to push himself upright in the rocker. He was not sure that he succeeded, but he tried. "Wha'zit?"

"It's here, sir." The kid dipped into his pouch and brought out a thin sheaf of envelopes, glanced through until he found the one he wanted and then handed it to Longarm.

"Do I . . . do I hafta sign for it or . . . anything?"

"I, uh . . ." The kid peered into Longarm's watery eyes and changed his mind about what he was going to say. "It's all right, sir. I'll take care of it."

"Yeah. Thanks. Thanks, kid." Longarm fumbled in his pants pockets trying to find a tip for the boy. That was the right thing to do, wasn't it? It took him a long time, and then all he could come up with was a tiny quarter eagle, a gold two-dollar fifty-cent piece. By then, though, the messenger boy had turned and gone. Longarm tried to return the coin to his pocket. He missed. It fell to the porch floor and rolled into a crack.

Longarm closed his eyes and rocked back and forth for a few moments, trying to get his head to stop swirling around like it insisted on doing.

Eventually—it might have been several minutes or several hours later—he sat forward and with some difficulty tore open the envelope.

The message was written in Henry's careful hand but signed by Billy Vail.

One single phrase glared up at him from the paper: "DISCHARGED FROM DUTY."

That was it then. Convicted of manslaughter and now he had been fired.

Billy wanted his badge back. After all these years, Billy was taking his badge away.

Longarm sat there. Devastated. A tall, lean, dark-haired

man, broad of shoulder and narrow of hip. A fine lawman . . . or used to be, they said. Just don't stand in front of him when he has a gun in his hand.

Billy Vail's best deputy. Or used to be, they said. Washed up now. Unemployed and without prospects.

Fired!

Longarm rocked slowly back and forth. Eventually his eyes drooped shut and his chin sank down toward his chest. The message form fluttered out of his fingers and fell to the porch floor.

Fired!

After all these years.

Private citizen Custis Long slept.

Chapter 2

The bitch. If he had seen her, he would have kept walking. Instead she was hiding inside the vestibule. When Longarm opened the front door and stumbled inside, he found himself face-to-face with her.

"I'm . . . in a hurry. We'll talk later."

"We will speak *now*, Mr. Long," his landlady snapped. "You are overdue with your room rent." She sniffed into her handkerchief. "Besides which, you have not been sober for weeks."

"I'm . . . fine." He was not. He had been drinking beer and playing cards all night, but he did not intend to admit that. "Fine," he repeated dully.

"You will pay me what you owe and a month in advance besides or I shall expect you out of my house within the hour."

"I can't . . . uh, can't . . ." Longarm looked up, recognizing after the fact that he and the lady were not alone in the vestibule. Someone was standing behind her. A man. In a blue uniform coat with brass buttons. Longarm blinked and tried very hard to focus his attention on the man. After a moment he smiled. "H'lo, Howard."

The cop scowled. "Don't be expecting any favors from me, boyo. I got a job to do here, and you're just another private citizen. You got that, Long? No favors. None."

"But Howard . . . you and me . . ."

"I mean it, Custis. No favors. You pay the lady or you get out."

"I got no place t' go."

"I am not without a heart," the landlady said. "You can put your things in my basement until you find another place to stay. But you must go, Mr. Long. You must go now."

"Go on, Long," Howard urged. "I don't wanta have to run you in for drunk and disorderly. You been given enough favors already when it comes to that. Go on now." Howard took him by the elbow and swung him back around toward the porch and the street beyond. The unexpected movement caused Longarm to lurch off balance. He fell to one side, crashed into the vestibule wall and spilled out the front door onto the porch.

He was very dimly aware of Howard's voice. "I'll take care of him, missus."

"Thank you, Officer."

Longarm felt someone turn him over and drag him to his feet. Howard, that was. Longarm smiled. Good man, Howard. Pleasant. Helpful.

"Come along, Long." Howard began pushing and pulling and half dragging him across the porch and down the steps. Out onto the street.

Longarm found himself sitting cross-legged at the base of an iron lamppost. He had no idea how he had gotten there or why his hand was chained to the post.

Fleeting seconds later a black-painted police ambulance stopped beside him.

Ambulance his lily white ass, Longarm thought trucu-

lently. Paddy wagon was another name for it. The police ambulances brought no succor to the ailing; they swept up the scum off the streets.

He tried to puzzle out why the police ambulance would have stopped here.

Ah, so the driver and bullyboy could speak with Howard. Of course.

Longarm was proud of himself for having worked that out.

He closed his eyes and did not even open them again when he felt himself being picked up and tossed through the air.

He landed heavily and rolled. It was dark where he was, and comfortable. He felt as if he were floating.

Longarm smiled benignly as the distant sound of rumbling wheels lulled him to sleep.

Chapter 3

Again? Would they be coming for him again, damn them? Longarm lay on the welded steel plate that served as a bunk. Behind the welded steel sheets that covered the walls. Except for the door and window openings, which had welded steel bars on them. He lay on the cold steel bunk and he trembled.

They would come again. He was sure of it.

Longarm heard the squeal of the heavy door leading to the offices beyond this holding cell. A guard wearing a blue uniform coat and khaki trousers sauntered in, whistling happily and swinging his truncheon in time with the tune. Longarm could almost—but not quite—remember the title of the melody. He knew he had heard it before, though. That was something.

Longarm raised his head to look. The movement caused pain. His muscles ached, and he was badly bruised. His ribs were battered, several probably broken, so that it hurt just to breathe. He winced.

The guard passed down the row of cells until he reached the last, the large holding cage where men were put to dry out or to await appearances before the magistrate. When he

got to the end of the row, the guard, a young fellow with a straggly mustache and curly hair, turned, still whistling, and started back the other way.

This time he did something that Longarm dreaded. He turned down the wicks of the lamps that hung on the wall. Five of them. They gave a good light when the flames burned high. Now the guard turned them down until they were almost, but not quite, extinguished.

The large room became dim, pockets of shadow turning the farther reaches of the cell block to utter darkness.

Longarm's trembling intensified. He knew what was to come.

Payback.

This was their opportunity. This was their chance to inflict on one of the hated lawmen some measure of revenge.

And cach night thus far thc occupants of thc holding cell had made the most of their opportunities.

The heavy door slammed shut. A moment later Longarm could hear the dull grind of the foot-long key being turned and the clunk of a heavy bar being set in place.

There was no sound of footsteps after that. The door was heavy enough to block almost all sound.

It started within seconds of the door being secured for the night.

"Remember me, Long? I remember you, you son of a louse-ridden bitch."

"I don't mind being in here now, Long. Hell, I'd pay to be behind these bars."

"We are gonna kick your nasty ass, Long."

"Again."

The voices came from every corner of the cell. There were seven or eight men in the cell with him. Too many for him to fight off.

He had managed it the first night. Fought until he was too exhausted to raise a fist or to kick another man in the gut.

They got to him the second night. And the third. And now they would pummel him again. He no longer had the strength to fight back. Worse, he no longer had the will.

They had defeated him. More than just physically. Night after night. Sick from too much cheap Injun whiskey. Hopeless and adrift.

The prisoners had won. Custis Long was beaten.

He lay on the steel slab and waited for the prisoners to come out of the shadows and once again do as they promised.

"We're gonna beat your stinking, hairy ass, Long. Beat you until you can't stand no more. Count on it."

And he knew it was the truth.

Chapter 4

"I am sorely disappointed in you, Longarm."

Tom Stead peered down from the judicial bench. He was not at all like the friendly, whiskey-drinking, cardplaying chap Longarm had spent so many evenings with in the past. "Disappointed, I tell you. Why, even after the long weekend you've barely sobered up enough to stand upright."

"Yes, sir." Longarm thought it pointless to mention to His Honor Tom that the reason he was hunched over was because he still hurt like hell from the nightly beatings he experienced in the cells. Tom would just think he was whining. Or, worse, seeking special favors.

"Bailiff, what is the charge here?"

"Drunk and disorderly, Your Honor."

Longarm knew the bailiff too. He used to play billiards with Matt Lunford now and then. Longarm glanced down at his battered hands. If he had a billiards cue in his hands now, he would use it to defend himself from the bastards in that cell. There was no way he could make himself steady enough to play the game.

Tom Stead looked down his patrician nose and sneered,

"Your stench suggests to me that the charge is well founded. Do you have anything to say for yourself, Longarm?"

"No, Your Honor."

"Nothing at all?"

"Just do whatever the fuck you're gonna do, Tom, so's I can get away from this shitty place."

Stead clouded up like he was about to bring rain down inside the courtroom. He smacked his gavel loudly on the bench, decided that was not loud enough and did it again harder. "Prisoner, you will mind your tongue," he barked.

Longarm swayed a little and did his best to remain upright. He closed his mouth and his eyes alike and stood waiting for this bullshit to pass. There were places he wanted to be and things he wanted to do, and this accomplished none of them.

"He has been in for how long, Matthew?"

"Four days, Your Honor."

The gavel banged down again. "I hereby sentence this prisoner to serve ten days in the city jail. He does get credit for time already served." Bang with the gavel, and Matt took Longarm by the arm to lead him away.

At least now that he had been before the judge and was serving a properly adjudicated sentence, he would be taken out of the holding cell and put in . . . Oh, God. He just realized.

In the main jail there were even more prisoners. And fewer guards to watch over them.

It was very likely to be worse for him for these next few days, not better. Once the guards closed the cell block for the night, he would be at the mercy of whomever other prisoners were nearby.

Matt led him out of the nicely appointed municipal courtroom, to the dingy corridors that led to the city jail.

Descending the stairs into the jail wing of the building was much like descending into the noise and the stink of Hell.

Longarm walked woodenly and without interest in the ugliness around him.

Six more days. Then he would . . . He did not know what the fuck he would do. Did not know and did not much care.

He put one foot in front of the other. Then repeated the action. For now that was all he had to think about. One foot. Then the other.

Chapter 5

Longarm drew a straw-filled mattress and a single woolen blanket from the supply room, and then under the watchful eye of a guard—a stranger armed with a hickory billy—he carried it and a loose, ragged gray uniform to a small room near the cells.

"Change here. Put your own clothes in this sack. No socks, no shoes, no hats, no gloves. Just the uniform pants and shirt. You don't wear nothing else. Understand? Nothing." The guard whacked Longarm in the belly with his nightstick just for emphasis. "Nothing."

The man turned his head and cupped his ear. "I didn't hear you. What did you say?"

"Yes, sir," Longarm mumbled. "Yes, sir."

The guard grunted, satisfied, and announced, "My name is Fredericks but you can call me 'sir.' " He laughed, apparently under the impression that he had made a joke. "Now get that shit on and let's go."

Unlike the holding cells above, the basement cells encompassed a large, open area with stacked rows of steel cells along one wall, the cells piled one row on top of the other.

A steel staircase led up from the floor to a narrow, railed balcony.

There were . . . he counted . . . eight cells on top, served by that balcony, and another eight below. Each cell had four bunks in it, those also stacked in pairs.

Prisoners milled around in the large, open area. Longarm could see others seated on their bunks inside the cells.

Fredericks took Longarm into a cell on the bottom tier. He pointed to one of the steel platforms that served as bunks and said, "This one is yours. During the day this mattress is supposed to be folded over on itself and laid here on the foot of the bunk just like you see on these here other bunks. Your blanket is to be folded and placed on top of the mattress. Are you paying attention?"

"Yes, sir. Folded."

"Right. During the day you can sit in here or out there in the dayroom. Meals are served out of a cart that comes around twice a day. If you miss the cart, you go hungry, so don't be asking for extra food. If you got to piss or take a shit, use the buckets down at the end of the dayroom there. There's no buckets to use at night, so learn to hold your piss or sleep in it. It don't make any difference to me."

"Yes, sir."

"Lights turn low and a final walk-through is made at nine o'clock. Make sure you're in your own cell when the guard comes around to lock you in. No exceptions."

"Yes, sir."

The guard turned and abruptly walked out. For a moment it seemed rude of the man that he had gone without saying good-bye or otherwise indicating a desire to leave. Then Longarm realized . . . he was a prisoner now. He was no more important to these people than a turd in a bucket.

He did not even have anything in here to smoke. Other

risoners out in the common area were smoking. Longarm knew better than to ask for a cigar or even a cigarette. He was a lawman. Had been a lawman. To these prisoners he would be the enemy still.

And tonight . . . At least there could be no more than three of them coming after him once the cell was locked and the guards gone for the night. Why, getting beaten up by just three of the bastards should be practically a relief after his nights in the transient cells.

He sat on the edge of his bunk and waited. Waited for the food cart. For his cellmates to show themselves. For lights-out and the next round of fisticuffs. But only against three of the bastards this time. Only three.

Chapter 6

The cell doors closed with a clash of steel and the grind of keys being turned. Then one by one the lamps were turned low. Moments after that there was a dull thump of weary footsteps and the guards withdrew with a final crash of the heavy steel door. If this lower part of the jail was run anywhere close to the way the transient cells were, that meant no guard would show his face again in the cell block before dawn.

Longarm determined that he might be taken—anybody could be—but the assholes would not take him easily. He shifted to the end of his bunk and clenched his fists until his knuckles stood out white and pale and his hands began to hurt.

There was little light in the cell. His cell mates were no more to him than dark shadows.

He heard the rustle of straw and saw dim shapes detach themselves from the other tier of stacked bunks, opposite his. If the man on the bunk above his was moving, Longarm could neither see nor hear any indication of it.

"You're Long, ain't you?" a gravelly voice inquired.

The fellow who had spoken looked behind him—checking to see that he was not alone probably—and moved closer.

Longarm ignored the man and the one who followed practically in that one's footsteps.

There was still no movement from the bunk above his. Perhaps the idea here was for them to draw him off his bunk, out into the open floor. Then the one above could drop down behind, and they would have him boxed in the middle of the three.

To the prisoner who was following so close behind the belligerent one, Longarm said, "You get any closer an' you'll be crawling up his ass. Or is that the idea, you cornholing son of a bitch?"

That made both of them mad—which was exactly what Longarm had in mind. The two rushed him, and Longarm leaped to meet their charge.

He was thoroughly tired of this bullshit and intended to take no more of it.

Longarm's fist slammed square into the face of the first one in line. The man's nose turned to red pulp, and blood sprayed ceiling-high.

Longarm followed that blow with a vicious, underhand punch to the pit of the man's belly. The breath whooshed out of him and he bent over, clutching himself.

The second man growled something Longarm could not understand—which was probably for the best anyway—and came ahead in a rush.

Longarm ducked under a wild punch and came up swinging. He battered the face of the prisoner with the heel of his right hand, lest he break his hand on the bony parts of the bastard's face, then bent low and delivered a quick tattoo of lefts and rights and lefts low on the man's belly.

Longarm thought about kicking each of them in the

nuts—they would have done as much for him, and he knew it—but remembered barely in time that the jailers had taken his boots away. Kicking one of them now was more apt to break his toes than to hurt these ignorant shits.

With both members of the frontal assault team at least temporarily disabled, Longarm spun around to face the third man, on the upper bunk behind him.

That fellow, however, was merely sitting cross-legged on the steel plate, observing the show with obvious interest.

"You ain't dealing yourself into this game?" Longarm asked.

The noncombative prisoner slowly shook his head. Then he said, "I guess it's true, what I heard."

"Depends on what you heard," Longarm returned.

"Heard they took your badge away and you was on your uppers."

Longarm sighed. "That's true enough, dammit."

One of the men on the floor dragged himself more or less upright and retreated to his own bunk. The other was still lying on the floor, quietly retching. Judging by the stink, that one had shit himself.

"You still drunk?"

"Shit, I wish I was. I been in here for . . . I forget. Three or four days now."

"You can get whiskey in here, you know," the prisoner said.

"No shit?"

"No shit. If you got money, you can get almost anything in here. Except pussy. You can get a blow job, but no pussy."

"Not that it matters," Longarm told him. "I think I'm broke."

"You don't know?"

Longarm shook his head. "Not for sure, but I think so."

"You want a drink?"

"Does a chicken have lips?"

"Huh?"

Longarm chuckled. "Sorry. I'm funning you just a little."

"Oh. So let me ask you again. You want a drink?"

"Damn straight I do."

"Here." The fellow untied the end of his mattress, fished around inside for a moment and produced a nearly full pint bottle. "Help yourself."

Longarm grabbed the pint before his benefactor might withdraw the offer. He jerked the cork out and had to exert all his will to keep from guzzling the entire bottle full. He permitted himself one sweet, fiery swallow, then another very small sip that he swished around in his mouth before swallowing it too.

Reluctantly he jammed the cork back into the bottle and returned it.

"How's about a cigarette now?" the prisoner offered.

"What are you, my new best friend?"

"You want one or not?"

"Damn right I do."

"Here's the makings and a block of matches. Help yourself."

Longarm clumsily rolled a cigarette—the flimsy papers produced a smoke that could not compare with a proper cigar, but they were damn sure better than nothing—and scratched a match aflame.

Lordy, but that did taste fine. The whiskey. Now a smoke too? Damn!

He stepped forward and handed the cloth pouch of shredded tobacco back to the man on the upper bunk, but the fellow was lying down faced away from the other occu-

pants of the cell. To all intents and purposes he seemed already to be asleep.

And Longarm did not so much as know the fellow's name.

Longarm unfolded his mattress, spread his blanket over it and lay down to sleep.

Chapter 7

The morning routine was logical enough. A pair of guards came down the hallway with a cart—the wheels squealed loudly, suggesting it was the same cart that would be used later to deliver food to the prisoners—carrying freshly filled lamps. The new lamps were lighted and hung, and the low-burning existing lamps were extinguished and placed onto the cart.

When all the lamps were burning bright, the cart was pushed out of the way and a whistle shrilled.

One guard, but only one, came inside the cell block. The other locked him in using a key that stayed outside the bars. The guard who was inside the cage started on the upper tier and moved down the cells one by one, unlocking the barred doors and swinging them open.

It was a simple enough system but sensible. The prisoners could easily overpower any one guard if they wished. But then what? They would still be locked inside the main cage, and the guard who stepped inside did not have the key to that.

No doubt the guards who remained outside were given instructions that should a takeover be attempted they were

not under any circumstances to go to the rescue of . friend. They should not unlock the cell-block door ever the inside guard's life was threatened.

Of course there would be some doubt as to whether the guards would actually follow that instruction if there was an uprising.

Not that Longarm anticipated one. Rising up off this steel bunk was about all he could manage after a fitful night of bruises and bad dreams.

When the inside guard reached their door, he glanced down at a work sheet on a clipboard and shouted, "Jake. Outside!"

"Yes, sir."

Longarm saw a pair of bony ankles swing down in front of his face. Then the prisoner who had refrained from joining in the fight dropped lightly to the floor.

"Gather up," the guard ordered. Whatever that meant.

"Yes, sir."

Longarm quickly enough learned the meaning of the phrase. Jake grabbed his mattress and a blanket off his bunk and slung them over one shoulder.

"Coming, sir." Nice and polite. Longarm was not sure he believed that, and probably the guard did not believe it either, but the words were spoken and the jail protocol observed.

Longarm was learning. This was a whole new world he was in now.

The prisoner known as Jake walked out of the cell without a backward glance for his cell mates.

As soon as he was gone, Longarm stood up. He discovered that Jake, bless his soul, had left an extra blanket behind. And that pint bottle wrapped securely with it. Longarm appropriated both to his own use and muttered a thank-you to the departed Jake.

is time when he walked out into the cell block, he did anding tall.

The other two assholes in his cell did not bother him again.

Chapter 8

"Long."

"Yo."

"Gather up."

"Yes. Sir." Longarm did not wait to be asked a second time. He grabbed up his mattress and one blanket—somebody else might want the extra that Jake had left behind—and headed for the cell-block door. He did not say good-bye to anyone; he had made no friends here.

"Stand over there. Keep your mouth shut."

Longarm had learned to follow instructions. He was told to shut up. He did. He did not even say thank you.

The guards locked and carefully checked the cell-block door, then motioned for Longarm to follow. Along the way they chatted back and forth as if he were not there. And in a manner of speaking he supposed he was not, at least not to them. To the guards he and all the other prisoners were scum. They deserved no consideration and they got none.

Longarm followed in silence with his mattress and one blanket draped over a shoulder.

The guards stopped outside a room with a sign over the door labeled "Supply." They motioned Longarm in. Once

he was inside, both of them left, leaving him with a wheezing old fart who looked like he might keel over and die from a heart attack at any moment.

"Name?" the old man asked.

"Long. Custis."

"Put the mattress and blanket over there. Wait here." The old guy shuffled slowly out of sight behind a rack of shelving. An interminable amount of time later he reappeared, moving even more slowly if that was possible. This time he was carrying a box.

He set the box down on the waist-high counter that separated them and took his time about producing a sheet of paper and transferring some information onto it from a different sheet. Then he turned it around and handed Longarm a pencil. "Sign here."

"This says you've delivered all of my personal effects," Longarm said.

"That's right."

"But I haven't seen what you have in the box."

"Do you want it or not? You don't sign, you don't get. Your choice."

Longarm signed. Reluctantly.

The old clerk shoved the box across the desk to him.

Longarm pulled the top flaps of the box open and peered inside. His clothing was there and his boots. So was his Colt, showing flecks of rust near the muzzle after sitting uncleaned on a Denver jail shelf.

There was no tweed coat. It took a moment, then Longarm remembered that he lost the coat somewhere weeks earlier. And the hat . . .

He pulled the limp, dust-covered black slouch hat out of the box. "What the fuck is this?" he demanded.

"Your hat. Whadaya think?"

"This is *not* my hat. When I walked in here, I was wearing a dark brown Stetson hat. Best quality beaver. Low, rolled crown. Four-inch brim. What happened to it?"

The old man shrugged. "I dunno anything about that. That's your box. Your stuff in it. You want to see the shelf ticket?"

"Listen, I don't know an' don't care shit about your stupid shelf ticket or whatever you want to call it. All I know is that this is not my hat. I want my hat."

"Mister, that right there is your hat now. You don't want it, leave it in the box. It don't make no difference to me." He sat down and began rummaging through his desk, obviously dismissing Longarm. After a moment he looked up and said, "You can leave now. Else I'll call the guards and have you arrested all over again for public disturbance."

"This isn't in public and I'm not disturbing anything," Longarm said. "I just want my hat."

"If I say 'tis, then 'tis. Now you either get your ass outa here or I'll invite you to stay for another ten."

Longarm could have snapped the old bastard's neck. And wanted to. Not that it would accomplish anything.

Making a distinctly sour face, he inspected the interior of the scruffy hat—damn thing might have had bugs in it for all he knew—and very gingerly put it on. It was an uncomfortably loose fit, falling down to rest on top of his ears when he let go of it.

"You look like shit," the old fart said.

"Thanks."

"That hat don't fit you."

Longarm gave the old fool a dirty look and strapped on his .45 Colt.

"Through that door there and turn right to get to the back alley."

"Why . . . ?"

"Been my experience that most of you like to go out by way of the alley. But you do whatever the hell you want. It don't make no difference to me." The old man went back to shuffling papers.

Longarm went through the door indicated. And turned right to get to the alley.

Chapter 9

Longarm could not remember if he had any cash in his pockets when he was arrested. If he did it was gone now, pilfered by some cop or jail employee.

He was stone-cold broke now and did not even have a room to go to, or any place to find a meal. He had to get some money. And fast.

The jail food had been barely adequate to sustain life, never mind satisfying or good-tasting. And the guards had pulled him out of the cell block before even that poor fare was served this morning. Now Longarm's belly was clenching and rumbling with hunger.

There were a few places in the city where he could likely beg for a bite to eat, places where he had dined often in the past and tipped well. Some of those surely would have given him a plate of scraps if nothing else. But Longarm still had some vestiges of pride left. Damned few perhaps, but some. He simply did not want to be seen begging in places where he was known. That would have compounded his humiliation.

He needed food and . . . he wanted a drink. Badly. His

mouth watered and hands trembled even at the thought of a tall, dark amber glass of rye whiskey.

He leaned against the brick wall in the alley behind the Denver jail and went through his pockets with all the care and concentration he could muster.

There was little enough in them. A dark blue kerchief, soiled and rumpled but not torn. His pocketknife. One dirty sock. Why the hell he would have a sock in his pocket, and only one sock at that, he could not begin to remember.

But money? Not a cent.

Come to think of it, he did not have his Ingersoll railroad-grade watch—surely he could have sold that for a dollar or two—or his watch chain with the .41 derringer soldered in place where a fob would normally be. Those items . . . gone. He did not bother trying to remember what might have happened to them. He did not have them now. That was all that mattered.

He had the boots, trousers, balbriggans and shirt he was wearing. And the miserable son of a bitch of a slouch hat on his head. Lord, he hoped that thing did not have lice or some other vermin hiding inside it.

And he had his Colt revolver. His fine, double-action, .45-caliber Colt revolver.

It was the only thing of any value that he still possessed.

With a grimace of resignation, Longarm left the alley and turned in the direction of Denver's skid row.

That was where a man could find the cribs of the cheapest whores, the lowest class of saloons . . . and the greatest concentration of pawnshops.

"Five dollars."

Longarm stared at the scrawny, unshaven, insulting wreck behind the counter. "I paid thirty-seven dollars for

at gun and another fifteen for the belt an' holster. Now you tell me they're only worth five?"

"I could maybe stretch it to seven, but that's my final offer. If you don't like that, try somewheres else."

Longarm in fact had already tried elsewhere along the row. The most he had been offered so far was $5.50. The pawnbrokers were a bunch of damned thieves, he was concluding. Someone ought to investigate them.

"I'll . . . Aw, shit. Eight dollars."

"I said seven. You want that or not?"

Longarm nodded. "Yeah, all right. Seven."

The fellow carefully shucked the fat, bright cartridges out of the Colt and dropped them into a cigar box that held an assortment of loose ammunition in half a dozen calibers or more, then laid the revolver on the shelf behind him. He took his time about bringing his cash box out—after first giving a nod to the shotgun guard who was posted on a platform overlooking the store—and counting out seven shiny silver dollars.

Longarm held his hand out to receive the money. They were heavy on his palm. They felt good in his pocket.

He had not had to worry about money for a very long time. Now he was already worrying about how to get more once this was gone.

His mouth watered in anticipation of a drink. There were three saloons on this block, and he was not known in any of them. There had been a time when they would have been too low in class for his trade. But this was not that time.

Just one drink. What would it cost? A quarter? Maybe less. Or he at least could get a beer. That only cost a nickel. A beer would settle the churning in his belly.

But . . . a beer would lead to a whiskey would lead to

getting drunk would lead to being broke again. He had start acting responsibly again.

What he really needed was food.

He knew where he could get a bowl of spicy beans for a dime. Forget the coffee to go with it. That would be another nickel. Hell, he might as well treat himself to a beer as buy a cup of coffee.

Longarm shook his head violently from side to side. He was feeling . . . tempted.

What he needed to do, dammit, was to go get those beans. Then a job. He had to find some way to support himself. Seven dollars would not last long, and after that was gone . . . then what?

Longarm headed out of skid row and started walking toward Aurora, Colorado, where the Mexican restaurants could be found.

Chapter 10

The stockyards. A man could nearly always find something to do in and around the cattle pens. Feeding, watering, keeping the cattle on their feet and moving—there was always something that needed to be done.

But, dammit, he was too well-known at the stockyards. In better days he sometimes hung out there, smoking and sharing a pint bottle and swapping yarns with the cowhands and railroaders and layabouts who drifted past.

For that matter, when he first came to Denver, before he had the great good fortune to find his niche in law enforcement, he'd found work in the stockyards.

He was a do-everything hand. Small wages but great friendships. He still remembered those days fondly.

Custis Long did not want to be recognized by any of the fellows he used to know. It was not so much that he was ashamed of his present unsavory circumstances—although in truth that played a small role too—but more that he did not, absolutely did not, want to be the object of any man's pity.

He had not fallen that damned far.

He ate his beans and was so hungry that he paid for a

second bowl as well. Twenty cents. He could not really afford such extravagance, but he needed to keep his strength up for . . . whatever.

There was a horse-drawn trolley that ran on tracks between Aurora and the city of Denver, but a ride on it cost five cents. It cost him nothing to walk back to the city.

In a seedy neighborhood he found a saloon where he was not known and stepped inside. The scents of beer and whiskey surrounded him, invited him to drink and to forget. Longarm resisted the temptation, but his throat tightened and his stomach lurched at the thought of a tall, dark glass of whiskey.

"What'll you have, mister?"

"I, uh, I was looking for a card game," Longarm stammered. He liked poker and thought he played well. In a place like this, surely the competition would be marginal at best. He could hold his own here. Likely could increase his poke a little.

"The table costs two bits an hour," the barkeep said.

"Done," Longarm told him.

"Two bits then. In advance."

Longarm dug into his pocket and forked over a quarter.

"You got a deck of cards?"

"No."

"That's five cents an hour extra."

"In advance?"

The barkeep nodded. Longarm went to his pocket again for the nickel.

"Marked or unmarked?" the bartender asked brazenly.

"I'll take 'em plain."

"Suit y'self." The man fetched a pasteboard box from under the counter and handed it to Longarm. "Thirty cents every hour. And mind, I'm timing you."

"I won't forget." Longarm carried the deck of cards to an empty table and sat down. He shuffled the deck—it was not quite new but did not look like it had been marked—and spread it on the table before him.

Several customers had been observing all this. They may have overheard Longarm specify that he wanted to play with unmarked cards. Two of them drifted near, then a third and finally a fourth.

"Set down, gents. Make yourselves comfortable." Longarm dropped his meager collection of silver dollars onto the table beside the cards. There might not have been many, but they rang nice and pretty.

Five hours later, Longarm walked out of the saloon with exactly one dollar and forty-five cents remaining in his pockets. His luck was lousy. Or possibly it was his judgment that was shot all to hell and gone.

"Thanks for the education," he told the other players as he gathered up the little money he had left and dropped it into his pocket. "The cards belong t' the house, by the way." He inclined his head toward the barkeep. "I expect he'll tell you when he wants them back."

Longarm headed out into the street. It was afternoon by then and the sun was rapidly sinking toward the distant mountain peaks. Longarm had no idea where he would sleep tonight or how he would keep warm once the chill of the night set in.

He started walking again, this time toward Cherry Creek and what used to be his home neighborhood. Back when he had a home.

Chapter 11

Longarm woke up shivering. He had only a half-rotten saddle blanket to sleep under and a tattered canvas shelter half to lie on top of, and those stiff, dirt-crusted pieces of cloth were not enough to keep a man's bones warm.

He sat up, plucked some twigs off the pile he had gathered the evening before and used the tip of one to probe the ashes of last night's fire. He found a coal, leaned down and patiently blew on it until he got the twig burning. With that for a start, he was able to build a tiny fire. It was not much of a flame—not that he had anything to cook anyway—but it was enough to warm his hands over and to give an illusion of heat.

Longarm sat like that until the fire burned out, then he climbed to his feet and shivered some more. Dammit, he wished that he at least had his coat back.

But then he might as well wish for a razor. And a steak dinner with all the fixings.

He probed a fingernail inside his dark, bushy beard, unshaven for more than a month now, and scratched. Scratching an itch seemed to be one of the few pleasures left to him. Perhaps it was a good thing that he had so many itches.

Which he hoped to hell came from the fact that it was so long since he'd bathed but had nothing to do with lice or other body vermin.

He was flat broke now. And hungry.

Actually he was past being merely hungry. He was becoming weak from lack of food. Lack of warmth. Lack of proper sleep.

He rolled his bedding, such as it was, and hid it in a shallow depression in the ground, then covered it over with last year's dead leaves.

So much for housekeeping.

With a sigh, Longarm waded across the shallow, trash-strewn creek and emerged onto the opposite bank. He needed a job. Any sort of job.

"Get out of here, you fucking bum." The man who stepped out of the back door was a beefy, heavyset son of a bitch who looked like he could use his chin whiskers for sandpaper and his hands as hammers. He was at least as tall as Longarm and probably outweighed him by sixty pounds.

Longarm glared at him. "You're a bouncer, not the boss. I want t' see the boss."

"How do you know I ain't the boss?" the big man demanded.

" 'Cause nobody as dumb as you could be the boss of anything more'n an outhouse."

"Why you miserable piece of shit. Let's see if you still want to say that when I'm done beating on you."

"That'll be the day," Longarm snarled.

The big, dark-haired bastard lunged forward. He threw a right hand that would have taken Longarm's head off if it connected. Longarm easily swayed backward away from the punch.

He sidestepped the bouncer's charge and gave the big man a light push between the shoulder blades when he rushed past. The push did exactly what Longarm wanted. It redirected the fellow's body just a bit and disrupted his balance.

Unfortunately—for the big guy—the new direction sent him speeding awkwardly, arms flailing, toward the edge of the back porch of the house. He was either going to plunge headlong onto the gravel below or drop painfully onto his knees. He chose to drop where he was.

The fellow landed with a thump and a roar of fury. He jumped to his feet, fists pumping even though he had no particular target in mind for them.

Longarm stepped back away from the human windmill. He stood poised lightly on the balls of his feet and waited for an opening. In the windows behind him he was dimly aware of the other occupants of the three-story house. They had gathered like so many twittering birds to watch the fight.

The big fellow got control of himself and quit throwing useless punches. "You cocksucker," he spat. "I'm gonna tear your head off and throw it in the creek."

Longarm said nothing. But when the big man moved forward, Longarm's rock-hard right first pulped the fellow's lips and mouth. The punch rocked him. His head snapped back and blood flew. Longarm stepped forward again.

He threw a hard, low left to the man's belly, then a right to the breadbasket. The fellow went pale and began to suck for air.

Longarm moved closer. His fists began to pound the big ape. Rights and lefts, singly and in combinations.

Blood flowed free and flew in all directions.

The big fellow began to wilt. He staggered and three times went down.

He only got up twice.

"I . . . I . . . I yield," he gasped.

"You yield? You fucking *yield*?" Longarm barked. "What's that supposed t' mean?"

"I mean . . . I mean you beat me, fella. I can't believe it, but you did. You whipped me. What's worse, you did it on the square. No tricks. You just whipped my ass."

Longarm offered a hand to help pull the beaten fellow to his feet.

"What . . . what did you want anyway?"

"I'm hungry," Longarm said. "I got no place t' live, nothing t' eat. I want a job."

"Come inside. I'll see you get something to eat." He stopped and audibly sniffed. "On second thought, you'd best stay out here on the porch. I'll bring you out a plate of food. And I'll talk to the boss about a job for you too. I'm thinking we could use another bouncer around here, and God knows you're qualified for the job. Wait here. I'll get your food and see what she says."

"She?"

"Uh huh. You got anything against working for a woman?"

"Friend, I'd work for the devil hisself if it would put food in my belly an' a roof over my head."

"This would be close," the big man said. "This is a whorehouse. Best one in the county, I'd say. Anything wrong with that?"

Longarm shook his head. He grinned. "Like I said . . ."

"By the way," the big fellow said, "my name is Sammy. Sammy Jahn, which is funny when you think about it because it's pronounced like I was a john in the whorehouse. But it's spelled a little different. And you?"

"Custis Long."

Sammy Jahn gave Longarm a quizzical look. "I'd heard . . ." He shook his head. "Never mind. If it don't matter to you, it don't matter to me neither. Wait here now. I'll go tell Mrs. Brighton about you."

Longarm sank gratefully onto a cane-bottom chair on the back porch.

Chapter 12

Ham, grits, eggs . . . they filled the hollows in Longarm's belly and warmed him through. A cup of steaming hot coffee finished the job. He had not felt that good in more than a month.

"Those clothes," Sammy said after Longarm's plate had been collected and taken back inside the kitchen. "They gotta be burned, Long. They're starting to rot."

"They're all I got, Sammy. I got nothing to change to."

"I'll see what I can find." He grinned. "Just don't be fussy, y' hear?" Sammy went inside. A few minutes later a black couple—a shy, slender girl who looked to be twenty or thereabouts and an older, graying man—came out dragging a washtub. The two of them carried pails of piping hot water from the kitchen to partially fill the tub, then added enough cold water to make the temperature bearable.

The man went back into the house. The girl stood beside the filled tub with a bar of yellow naphtha soap in one hand and a scrub brush in the other. "Well?" she demanded.

"Well what?" Longarm countered.

"You gonna get in this here tub so's I can wash you or not?"

"I can't . . . I mean . . ."

"Mister, I done seen most everything a body could," she said. "You aren't gonna scare me an' nothing you got is gonna make me blink. Now get them rags off of you and hunker down in this here tub before the water gets cold."

Longarm stripped off what was left of his clothing and lowered himself cross-legged into the water. The water was hot and wonderful.

He was aware that the occupants of the house were at the windows again. But hell, the whores were not likely to be offended by the sight of a naked man. Or excited by it.

And oh, that bath did feel fine. Between that and his breakfast, he was commencing to feel downright human again.

By the time the girl was finished vigorously scrubbing and rinsing him, Longarm practically glowed. Sammy came back onto the porch with a big Turkish towel and a selection of clothing. "Try these," he said. "See what you think."

Longarm ended up with a pair of denim trousers and a red and black checkered shirt that he suspected belonged to Sammy. The jeans were too big in the waist, but a belt cinched down tight took care of that.

"We don't have any spare shoes laying around, but we can measure your foot and send Honey out to find you some," Sammy said.

"Honey?" Longarm asked.

Sammy grinned and pointed at the black girl, who was standing there waiting to carry the unneeded clothing back inside. "She's named that because when she was little she

was the color of honey. She's darkened up since then, but the name stuck."

Longarm reached up to tip his hat. "Pleasure t' meet you, Honey."

The girl dropped into a curtsy and bobbed her head but said nothing.

"I expect you're as presentable as you're going to get," Sammy said. "Come inside and meet the boss. Then we'll see if you've got the job or not."

The boss was younger than Longarm would have expected. She was a heavy, baby-faced woman who probably was still in her thirties. She had a stern, no-nonsense expression when she looked Longarm over, shoeless and wearing ill-fitting clothing.

"So," she said at length. "You are the famous Longarm I've heard so much about."

"No, ma'am," Longarm said. "I used t' be Longarm. I'm just plain Custis Long nowadays."

The woman grunted and nodded.

"What do you expect here?" she asked.

"I don't expect anything."

"What can you do for me?"

"Whatever you need, ma'am."

"Sammy says you can fight. And we already know you can shoot. What about your drinking?"

So she had heard about that too. Dammit! "I haven't had a drink in more'n a week," Longarm said. "I'm cold sober now. I don't have a problem with drinking interfering with my job. When I have a job, that is."

"You were fired from your last job because you were too quick to shoot someone. I don't need for my patrons

to worry about whether they will be shot if they come here."

"I understand that, ma'am."

"If I take you on, I want it clear to you that you only throw someone out if I want him out. You only shoot if I want someone shot. You do nothing on your own. If one of my gentlemen beats up one of my girls, you stay clear unless I tell you otherwise. It just may be that he has paid for that pleasure and is entitled to beat her without interference from you. Is that understood?"

"That might not be s' easy but . . . yes, ma'am. I step in on your orders only."

"But if I tell you to shoot someone, then you shoot them. No hesitation and no questions asked. If I order it, there will be no police report and no charges can be filed against you. Is that clear?"

"Yes, ma'am."

No charges and not even a police report? Wasn't that damn-all interesting, Longarm thought.

"Sammy is my senior bouncer, but there are times when he needs a night off. There is not normally a problem that one good man cannot handle, but it is possible. We used to have two bouncers, but one is in prison." She scowled. "He committed crimes that were not ordered by me. That was his mistake. I trust you can refrain from making that same mistake."

"Yes, ma'am."

The woman shifted her attention to Sammy Jahn, who was standing close by. "Give him Court's old room, and find him some shoes and a pistol. I'll trust you to show him the ropes around here." She looked back at Longarm. "My name is Cleo. Miss Cleo to you. Now go with Sammy. I have work to do here."

“Yes, ma’am, Miss Cleo, and . . . thank you, thank you very much.”

Miss Cleo sniffed and looked down at a ledger on the table, dismissing Longarm from mind.

Chapter 13

Nothing—not beating his meat when he was a kid or pussy when he got older or the taste of the best whiskey he'd ever had—nothing beat the feel of that bed.

Longarm's room was not much bigger than a decent wardrobe, but the bunk had a mattress on it and what more could a fellow need or want than that? After sleeping on a bed of rocks beside Cherry Creek, this felt like lying on top of a cloud.

He would happily have slept even longer, but Sammy tapped on the door to wake him and then came in without waiting for a response. "Wake up. It's almost six, and you and me got to get around."

The big fellow grinned when he brought something out from behind his back. "I got something for you."

Sammy handed Longarm a pair of heavy, lace-up linemen's boots and two pairs of woolly socks.

"Damn, Sammy. Thanks."

"Huh uh. I didn't pay for them. Miz Cleo did. She talks rougher than she really is."

"But how'd you get some that fit so good?" Longarm asked as he pulled the left boot on.

"Honey snuck in here while you was sleeping. She measured your foot and then went to find the boots. I guess they aren't exactly new. If that matters to you."

"Hell, no. They fit good. That's what counts. Where is Honey?"

"Her and Bill will be downstairs in the kitchen. You and me are fixing to go down there to get our breakfast. Then we can start the day."

"All right. Who is Bill?"

"He's the black fella you saw yesterday. He's the cook. Butler too, I suppose. Honey's the maid. She cleans up and helps the ladies dress, whatever else is needed around here."

"Bill is Honey's husband then?"

Sammy laughed. "Not hardly. Bill is Honey's daddy. He's the one who tells the story about what color she was when she was a baby. I sure as hell haven't been around here that long."

Longarm grunted and finished lacing up his new boots. He stood and stamped his feet a few times to settle them inside the leather, then he grinned.

"Good?" Sammy asked.

"Real good," Longarm said.

"Come on then. Let's go downstairs and get something to eat. Stores and . . . other outfits will start closing pretty soon, and the gentlemen could start coming along anytime after that."

"You hesitated for a second there. What kind of 'other outfits' did you have in mind, Sammy?"

But the big man only shook his head. "You'll see. If you pay attention and know what's what, you'll see."

Longarm shrugged and followed Sammy down to the kitchen, at the back of the house.

• • •

Twenty minutes later Sammy pushed his chair back and stood up. "Had enough?"

Longarm nodded. "I'm full up." He patted the top of his head and smiled. He didn't know about anything else, but Bill could damn sure do himself proud with ham and eggs and grits.

"Then let's go. It's our job to put the parlor in order before the gents start arriving. First thing is to stock the liquor cabinet. There's no bartender here. Guests can help themselves to whatever they want. We make sure there's enough for them to choose from.

"I'll show you how to judge what needs to be replaced . . . Miz Cleo doesn't like the bottles to stay in the cabinet once they get down to a third full or so . . . Then after you figure out what you need, you go see Miz Cleo in her office. She has the keys to the liquor storage closet. You tell her what you want and she'll give it to you."

Longarm nodded. "That seems simple enough."

"It is. Just make sure the gents don't run out of anything they want. That would be bad for business."

"All right."

"Same thing with the cigar safe and tobacco humidor. Keep them full. I'll show you where the tobacco supplies are kept. Those aren't locked up, by the way, and if you want something to smoke you can help yourself. She won't mind."

Longarm's mouth watered at the thought. It had been so long since he'd had a cigar . . . "She wouldn't mind? Are you sure?"

Sammy chuckled and took the lid off a tall glass humidor with a tight-fitting cork lid. "Here."

"Damn, man. D'you know what this is?" Longarm said with a huge grin.

Sammy shrugged. "They're all the same to me."

Longarm used the tools that were offered along with the humidor. He carefully trimmed the twist off, warmed the wrapper leaf with one match and then let the sulfur burn off a second match before using it to light the Hernandez y Hernandez panatela. When he drew the smoke gently into his lungs, he was fairly sure he must have died and gone to heaven.

"Come along now. Let me show you how we keep track of what girls are available and how you point a gentleman at a second choicc in case the girl he wants is already busy or something."

Longarm dutifully followed where Sammy led, listening and watching along the way.

Chapter 14

Longarm was amazingly tired come the dawn. Amazing because he had hardly done a thing the whole night long, yet he was sleepier and more worn out than if he'd been breaking rocks all night.

His job here mostly consisted of sitting on his butt, ready to jump if he was needed, and smiling whenever one of the gents walked past. It was the inactivity that exhausted him, strange though that seemed.

None of the guests recognized him, but he had known several of them. Of course his appearance was not what it used to be. As a deputy marshal he was clean-shaven except for his handlebar mustache, and he nearly always wore a snuff brown Stetson, corduroy trousers and tweed coat. And of course there was the big Colt in a cross-draw rig.

Here he was wearing a full beard, jeans and black slouch hat. Besides, no one would likely expect to find former deputy Custis Long working as a bouncer in a whorehouse.

And expectation is a great camouflage. People tend to see what they expect to see. Or want to see. The unusual quite often escapes them completely.

As for the gentlemen who patronized Miss Cleo's upscale whorehouse, Longarm saw a judge, an assistant police chief and several lawyers whom he recognized.

He had no idea how much each of the gents had to pay for their pleasures, but it must have been considerable, especially for the "special" services available from a few of the girls.

"For the right price, we do anything. Anything," Miss Cleo proclaimed with pride. "But only what is agreed to, only what is paid for. The code word is 'queen of England.' If you hear a girl shout that, you come running because she is in trouble or her gentleman is insisting that he get more than he paid for. Your job then is to straighten him out. But don't be hurting the guests."

"What if the guest is hurting the girl?"

"I can always find more girls. Gentlemen who can afford to come here are harder to replace."

Longarm nodded. "I understand."

"I hope you do."

Now, with daybreak soon on them, Longarm was exhausted. He trudged up the stairs to his tiny room and sank gratefully onto the side of his bunk. He unlaced his boots and kicked them off, then undressed and stretched out on top of the down comforter he had been given.

It felt so very . . .

He heard a muted, metallic click just outside his room. Longarm's hand flashed to the bedpost where his gunbelt was hanging.

The door pushed open with a faint squeal.

Longarm thumbed the hammer back on the Peacemaker and aimed it toward the door.

Whoever or whatever came in would be facing a hail of .45 slugs.

Chapter 15

"Oh, my God! D-don't shoot." The girl's voice was high-pitched and squeaky with fear.

Longarm quickly dropped the muzzle of his Colt, then eased the hammer down to the safe cock notch. "Is something wrong?"

She peered down the hallway behind her, then slipped inside his room and closed the door, leaning back against it as if she had had a long, hard night. Likely she had.

"I just . . . I was thinking." She paused.

"You was thinking what?" He shoved the Peacemaker back into the old holster Sammy had scrounged for him and returned it to the bedpost.

"I was thinking . . . I mean . . . I saw you. When you got your bath." She moved forward, close enough that he could smell the mixture of sweat and powder that covered her. She was wearing a blue silk wrapper. It gaped open beneath some very carelessly tied ribbons. Her body was pasty white and soft but not bad. Her tits hung heavy behind the silk covering. He could see the outline of her nipples against the cloth. She had long, dark, curling pubic hair below and brassy blond above. Her face was small and her eyes set too close

together. She had a small, delicate nose and generous mouth. Longarm thought she was reasonably pretty. He guessed her to be somewhere in her late twenties.

"You got one helluva big dick, you know?"

"I know," he said. "What of it?"

"Well, I just . . . I was with three men tonight. All of them old farts. Two of them thought they was God's gift to womankind. Which is funny because neither one of them could last more than a minute. All they knew was to stick it in and wiggle it around a few times. Then it was 'thank you, ma'am, see you next time' and reach for their clothes.

"The last was the worst. I don't know how old he was, but he looked old enough to be my grampa. Him," she made a sour face, "he couldn't get it up enough to stick it in to begin with. I tried. Lord knows I tried and tried. Rubbed my tits all over him. Sucked that limp old pecker and licked his balls until my jaw hurt, but he never did get off. A little cum dribbled out but I don't know that it did him much good. Old bastard kept me at it until Miz Cleo tapped on the door to tell me time was up. Even though he wasn't. Old fart," she growled. "And let me tell you something else. Those two quick-on-the-trigger assholes who did get hard-ons? Neither one of them had a dick as long as this finger right here." She held her middle finger up in the classic sign of disrespect.

"Why are you telling me all this?" Longarm asked.

"Like I said, I seen what you have." The girl—he was trying to remember her name, but if he'd ever heard it he could not remember it now—untied the ribbons on the front of her robe and let it fall completely open. She shrugged her shoulders and the silk slithered to the floor at her feet. "Those old bastards just got me warmed up, you see. I mean . . . I'm here because I like to fuck. It feels good. It pleases me.

But those teeny-dick gents . . . all they did was make me hot. I still need a man to, what you might call, bank the fires. So I was thinking . . ."

She leaned down as if to kiss him, then abruptly straightened. "I forgot to tell you. Before I come over here, I douched. I washed my pussy and took an enema and cleaned my mouth real good. I didn't think you'd be wanting sloppy seconds. Though if I'm wrong about that, just let me know and next time I'll leave everything be."

"Uh . . . next time?"

The girl giggled and leaned down again. This time she did kiss him, open mouth and busy tongue.

It had been a hell of a long time since Custis Long was with a woman, any woman, and this one was plenty warm and plenty willing.

He reached up. Curled one arm around her waist and pulled her down to the bed without breaking the kiss.

He kneaded her tits and rolled one nipple and then the other lightly between his thumb and forefinger. The girl moaned. Her nipples were hard as stone and stood up high and proud.

Her hand crept down his body, found his hard cock throbbing, lightly bouncing with each surge of blood through the massive tool.

"Nice," she whispered into his ear.

Longarm slid his hand between her legs. She was dripping wet there, droplets of her juice clinging to her pussy hair.

"Raise up a second, lover."

He did, and the girl moved deftly beneath his hips, positioning herself on her back, ready to receive him.

Longarm accommodated her desire. He lowered himself onto her as she reached between them to guide him in.

She gasped when he filled her. Longarm damned near gasped aloud himself.

It felt so good. Inside her body. Surrounded by warm flesh.

He pushed in deep, allowing her time to adjust to his size.

Then he began to rock slowly back and forth. In and out.

He had thought before that being on a soft mattress was the best feeling ever. He'd been wrong. This was. How the hell could he have forgotten that rather lovely fact?

"Do me, lover. Do me," she whispered.

Longarm was delighted to comply.

Chapter 16

It wasn't easy trying to ignore the squeals and sharp reports—slaps? spanking? something like that—that came from down the hall. Room 4, he thought. Or 5.

Longarm tilted his head to listen, smiled once as one of the paying guests walked past, then listened again. Sammy was seated at the small desk that was the bouncer's station. He too was listening to the fracas down the hall.

"Shouldn't we . . . ?" Longarm began.

Sammy shook his head no. They shouldn't.

Then they heard it. The girl in that room—that exquisitely pretty little Mexican with no tits, the one who liked to dress as if she were a child in pigtails—shrieked again, this time following the cry with a shouted "queen of England."

Both Longarm and Sammy responded, Sammy jumping up from the desk and Longarm launching himself down the hallway. Longarm reached the door to number 4 first. He flung it open and barged in.

"Sorry, folks." He touched the brim of his hat and backed up, crashing into Sammy, who was coming full-speed behind him. On the bed in number 4 were the girl with long, red hair and a gent with oiled, slicked-back black hair.

Longarm did not think either one of the pair missed a stroke as a result of his intrusion.

He pulled the door closed and followed Sammy to number 5. This time it was Sammy who went in first, and he went in fast. Longarm was on Sammy's heels.

The girl's name was Immaculata, known inside the house as Mac. She was curled in a tight ball on the floor. The john, a white-haired old goat, was standing over her. Both were naked. Mac's pigtails were unraveling, and she had bright red welts on her ass. The man had been using his belt on her. Among other things.

Mac's face was mottled red and purple, and both eyes had been blackened. The corner of her mouth was torn and running blood. As soon as she saw the bouncers, she started babbling in Spanish, the words tumbling out one practically on top of the others.

Sammy turned to Longarm. "Do you speak Spanish, man?"

Longarm shook his head.

Sammy asked the girl, "Slow down now, Mac."

"Are you talking to me?" the john demanded loudly.

"No, sir, not at all," Sammy said politely. "That's her name. Short for Immaculata."

The john huffed and puffed a little. Then when Mac sat up, he quickly kicked her in the pussy. Mac screamed again and fell over sideways, clutching herself with both hands.

Sammy and Longarm quickly flanked the john and took him, gently but firmly, by the elbows. They pulled him back away from Mac.

"Take your hands off me," the john barked. "Do you know who I am?"

"No, sir," Sammy said. Longarm knew. But he said nothing.

"I am . . ." He abruptly stopped, then a moment later said, "Never mind." He swung around to face Sammy. "I paid good money for this whore. I can use her however I wish."

"If Miz Cleo says so, yes, sir," Sammy said agreeably. "Custis, ask the lady to come here, would you please?"

Miss Cleo was downstairs. She came in a hurry when Longarm beckoned to her. He briefly explained the situation on their way back up the stairs.

The owner of the house was scowling in the hallway but all smiles and conciliation when she stepped inside number 5. She listened patiently to the john's not necessarily truthful explanations, but did not invite any comments at all from Mac. When the john was done talking, Miss Cleo was still smiling.

"Now, you know the rules, Harold. You are allowed anything you pay for but nothing more than that, and you paid to slap her around a little. You did not pay to damage her. I'm afraid I will have to add a great deal to your bill tonight. I expect you to pay for what you did to the girl, plus I expect you to pay a hefty fine."

"I do not think . . ."

"I have no way to enforce the fine, Harold, but I have friends who would be annoyed. And you would no longer be welcome here until the amount is met."

"For a little bitch like this?" he asked.

"Yes, Harold. Even for a little bitch like this one if she is my property. Now, do you want to pay the fine or not?"

"I . . . I'll pay."

Miss Cleo's smile was one of sheer delight. "Thank you, Harold."

"What about the girl? Can I finish with her now?"

"Yes, of course. Immaculata, dear, the gentleman is

permitted to do whatever he wishes with you now. Do you understand that, dear?"

The trembling and bright tears rolled down her cheeks. But she nodded her head. "*Sí señora.*"

Back at the desk Longarm tried to close his ears to the screams coming from room 5.

"So we're here t' enforce the money rules, not t' protect the girls, is that it?"

"Look, there's things you should understand," Sammy said. "One of them is that there's things you don't *want* to understand. Do you take my meaning?" He shrugged. "Anyway, Mac will get a vacation out of it while she heals up. Miz Cleo is good about that sort of thing."

"Jeez, I'm glad she's actually good about *some*thing," Longarm mumbled.

"Stick around, Custis. You'll learn." Sammy shrugged again. "Anyway, anyplace but here Mac is just a fifty-cent whore. Maybe less with that lousy shape of hers. But here she earns a straight five dollars for each gentleman plus bonuses for extra services. Like with this asshole tonight. Hell, she'll probably come out of this with fifty dollars or so."

"And if he ends up killing her?"

"Aw, that ain't going to happen."

"No, I suppose not. Thank goodness," Longarm said.

"Say, would you do me a favor?"

"Sure. Name it."

"Go down and tell Honey the supply closet is running low on towels. And bring some more vinegar up with you when you come back,"

"Uh, all that vinegar, what's it used for?" Longarm asked.

"You don't know? I'm surprised. They mix it into some

water and douche with it. Cleans 'em right out, they say, and helps keep them from getting knocked up too."

"I'll be right back," Longarm said, heading for the stairs to deliver the message to Honey and bring back another jar of cider vinegar.

Chapter 17

"Good morning, lover." The girl—he had learned that her name was Janie, but here she called herself Sheila—giggled and came into his arms. She liked to be kissed, cuddled, whispered to. As he had also learned. This early morning, after-work visit was becoming a regular thing. Too regular, actually.

Longarm loved pussy, pretty much all pussy, but a man who works in a steakhouse may want a piece of chicken every now and then. Besides, it was strictly against the rules for the help to be fucking one another. But he knew for sure that there were at least two pairs of girls who went at each other during their off-duty time, and that Bill was fucking one of the white girls. That was a remarkably brave thing for him to do, because even in Denver in this day and age he could wake up one morning hanging from a cottonwood tree if certain parties ever learned about it.

A bouncer knows his place, though. And a large part of that place is to keep his fool mouth shut.

Except right now. He opened it to admit Janie's tongue and poked his into her equally eager and receptive mouth.

She had been sucking on something—other than a dick, that is—probably a butterscotch caramel. She tasted good.

Her tits did not feel bad either, lying heavy in his hand. He rubbed a little, squeezed a little, gave her time to build up steam.

He was just reaching down to tug the ribbons that held her robe closed when he heard a light tapping at the door.

Both of them froze. If they were discovered together, it was possible they both would be fired.

"Coming."

Longarm backed away and held a finger to his lips. He motioned toward the wardrobe, which was no wider than a gun cabinet, and Janie slipped inside it. He pushed the door closed on her. He did not have to warn her to keep her mouth shut in there.

"Yes?" he asked as he opened the room door.

It was only Honey standing in the hallway. "Miz Cleo wants to see you."

Longarm heard a muffled sneeze coming from the wardrobe. Honey looked in that direction, then back at Longarm. He looked down at her with a sheepish grin and shrugged. Caught. Neither of them said anything, but he thought he could see a faint hint of smile pull at Honey's lips.

"Right away," he said.

He pushed the door closed long enough to release Janie from the wardrobe, then headed out into the hall and down two flights of stairs to the ground floor. He paused outside Miss Cleo's office door and knocked.

"Come in."

"Honey said you wanted to see me, ma'am."

"Bill has to go to the market over on Langley Place. Do you know it?"

"The produce market there? Yes, of course."

"He needs to bring some things back here. I want you to go with him. You can each push a hand truck. Between them those should carry everything he needs right now."

"Yes, ma'am."

She paused as if expecting Longarm to say something more. He stood patiently waiting to be dismissed.

"You aren't going to say anything?" she asked after a moment.

"No, ma'am. Should I?"

"It is just . . . some white men wouldn't want to be seen with a black, especially when the black man is the one in charge. That doesn't bother you, Long?"

"Ma'am, I hadn't actual thought about it. An' if I did take a minute t' study on it . . . no, I don't reckon it bothers me."

"All right. Good. Go on now. Bill is in the kitchen. You can each take a hand truck from the shed in back. He will show you what to do after that."

"Thank you, ma'am." He left, closing the office door behind him, and headed for the kitchen in the back of the house. He thought about going upstairs to his room to get his hat and revolver, but . . . dammit . . . it had been a very long night and those stairs seemed to get higher and steeper every time he went up them. And they were just going to the farmers' market. He left the hat and Colt where they were in his room and continued on back to the big kitchen.

Bill was there waiting for him. So was Honey.

"You going with me?"

Longarm nodded.

Bill kissed his daughter on the forehead, which seemed fine with her, then when she turned to go off about her own

business, he patted her on the butt, which was not all right. Honey whirled around and squealed, "Papa!" Bill winked at Longarm and headed out onto the back porch with a satisfied grin.

Longarm followed dutifully along behind.

Chapter 18

The produce market was a lively, vibrant place, even—or especially—at this predawn hour. Voices babbled in half a hundred accents. Iron tires ground heavily on the stone underfoot, the wagons and carts pulled by mules, by horses and by men. Longarm saw several milk carts being pulled by goats and one by the biggest damn dog he ever laid eyes on.

The scene was brightly lighted by lanterns hanging from cables while below them lay mounds and bins and baskets of every foodstuff imaginable, from cabbages to melons to zinc tubs of oysters packed in ice and rushed halfway across the continent by rail.

Slabs of beef, fresh pork shoulders, hams and bacon dangled from hooks, while close by live chickens and ducks loudly complained about their confinement in tiny wooden cages, and over them hung birds already killed and plucked.

Dozens of vendors mingled with scores of buyers, all of them striving to make the best bargains they could manage. Longarm was fascinated.

He followed close behind Bill, each of them pushing a hand truck with empty crates stacked up, crates that needed

to be filled with whatever Bill thought would be good to feed the ladies and treat the johns.

"All you have to do is push. I'll do all the buying. Do not try to help me. I know what I'm doing here," Bill cautioned.

"Fine by me."

Some of the men around them, men who were buying for many and perhaps even most of Denver's restaurants and cafes, sought the lowest price they could manage. A few, including Bill, looked for the best possible quality, price being secondary.

"All right, that takes care of the meats," Bill said once Longarm's hand truck was loaded. "Now we go over on that side. I need some eggs and other fixings. I'll order the breads and pies and sweetmeats. They'll deliver those later on."

Longarm nodded and set off behind the black man.

"Finally found your right place in life, did you, Long? Pushing a hand truck an' acting as a hey-boy to a nigger. Thank God I have lived to see this day." The voice was loud and unpleasant, and Longarm whirled to meet the taunt.

"Oh. It's just you, Rodney." Police constable Rodney Harrington liked to be called Harry but would answer to Rod as well. For some reason he despised the name Rodney. Which was why Longarm called him that. The two were not friendly. Never had been. Never would be as far as Longarm was concerned. "I thought it was an actual person speakin' to me. Now I see I was wrong about that."

Bill, who had been forging on ahead, noticed that his helper had stopped. The cook paused, turned. He started to speak, then seemed to reconsider, perhaps thinking that anything he might add would only make things worse. For, after all, Constable Harrington *was* the law here. A bawdyhouse cook and his helper had to tread lightly.

"I heard about you, Long. I knew it was only a matter of time before you got your comeuppance." Harrington squared off in front of Longarm as if daring him to say or do anything. Anything at all. "Well, Long? Are you gonna smart-mouth me? Are you?"

Longarm wanted to paste the son of a bitch in the face. Just one good shot with the right hand and Constable Rodney Asshole would be out cold. Longarm knew he could do it. He had done it once before. Rodney would be remembering that right now, he figured.

He wanted to.

He couldn't.

That would be assaulting a police officer, and that was a crime punishable by up to three years in the old territorial prison in Canon City.

Longarm took a deep breath. And lowered his eyes.

"Got nothing to say, Long? You fucking coward. Now that you got no badge, you're a fucking coward."

Longarm was trembling. Not from fear. Trembling with the effort of holding himself back.

Then Rodney raised his hickory nightstick.

Longarm saw the movement and glanced up. He saw the nightstick begin to descend toward the unprotected crown of his head.

You can kill a man that way. Rodney did not appear to think about that. Or perhaps he simply did not care.

The nightstick swept down.

Instinctively, without taking time for conscious thought, Longarm's arm flew high to block the blow.

The nightstick slashed hard onto Longarm's right forearm. He heard the thud of the baton striking flesh and an accompanying *crack* of breaking bone.

White-hot pain shot up his arm and into his shoulder,

and he had to grind his teeth hard together to keep from crying out. He did not want to give Rodney that satisfaction.

"That's it, Long. You tried to hit me. I'm taking you in." Harrington grabbed him by the arm—the right arm, the broken one—and pulled. Pain—so bad it curdled his gut and weakened his knees—shot through every pore of Longarm's body. He refused to cry out, though. Dammit, not a sound. Not one.

Harrington jerked Longarm's broken arm around behind his back, brought the left arm around too and clamped handcuffs onto him. The pain in his arm was so bad that Longarm was almost unaware of what else Rodney was doing to him.

The blue-coated copper shifted his grip to Longarm's upper arm—that was at least a little better—and pulled him along. "You're going to jail, you son of a bitch. That's where you belong."

Once again Longarm found himself chained to a lamppost, awaiting the arrival of a paddy wagon to haul him in along with the rest of Denver's garbage.

The Negro cook said nothing and quickly took himself well away from this trouble, leaving Custis Long on his own.

Chapter 19

There were a dozen men in the big holding cell, waiting to be tried, waiting to be taken to the city's cells, waiting to be transferred to Canon City, simply . . . waiting. Luckily for him, no one recognized the disheveled prisoner with the busted wing as their old enemy Custis Long. No one recognized him as the man who once was Billy Vail's top deputy.

Longarm wanted to keep it that way. With only one hand and his boots to defend himself with, a swarm of prisoners could jump his ass and beat him into the ground without breaking a sweat.

He shoved his right hand into the waistband of his jeans to keep the arm from flopping around and hurting any worse than it already did, then wedged himself into a corner with his right shoulder tight against cold stone. At least no one could come at him from that direction. He would be able to hold his own a little longer that way.

But the best thing was that no one recognized him. He kept it that way right up until late afternoon when the cell was busy with prisoners who were coming and going. Longarm figured his turn before the judge had to come

soon. After that he would be taken down to the cells for however long his sentence turned out to be.

It would be better down there. More guards and fewer other prisoners to defend against when the guards were absent.

Through the bars of the holding cell Longarm saw Rodney Harrington strolling cockily down the aisle, rattling his nightstick along the steel like a kid running a stick along a picket fence. Harrington certainly knew how to draw attention to himself. And scowls, curses, even a little spit from those toward the back.

"Custis Long," Harrington loudly announced. "Longarm. I just wanted you to know what's happening with your case. I have an important meeting this afternoon."

Longarm grimaced. The last time Rodney Harrington had an important meeting was when his mother gave birth to him. More likely the bastard had promised to meet a crony who owed him a drink, or a new whore in the cribs who was going to drop her drawers for him.

"The judge has agreed to hold your trial over until tomorrow's docket, so it looks like you'll be in this cell overnight. I just wanted you to know that, Longarm. As a professional courtesy, you understand. One law officer to another, like."

Then, smiling and obviously quite pleased with himself, Constable Harrington turned and left the cell area.

Longarm's fellow prisoners turned too. To stare at their fellow inmate. The one with the broken arm.

Thank you ever so fucking much, Officer Harrington, Longarm thought.

The other prisoners began crowding closer. Ever closer.

Longarm balled his one good fist and waited. Left hand,

feet . . . and teeth. He had forgotten about his teeth, but he could bite the sons of bitches once they got close enough to take him down.

He braced himself for what was about to come.

Chapter 20

"Good Lord! What in hell happened to you?"

Longarm smiled. Anyway tried to. It felt like his face was breaking apart when his lips moved.

He was . . . a mess. His left ear was torn and bleeding. There was a deep cut open over his left eye and another on top of his scalp. He hurt in every bone and muscle in his body. He had taken the worst beating of his life and looked every bit of it.

"What about the other guy?"

"Guys," Longarm said. "There were . . . I dunno how many of the son o' bitches."

"They beat you good."

Longarm managed a grin and to hell with the pain. "They weren't getting no virgin. There's some hurtin' boys back in that cell too." He paused to take a deep breath. "Anyway . . . it's nice t' see you, Sammy. How'd you get me out? Ain't that against the law?"

"Miz Cleo called in some markers," Sammy Jahn said. "She got right on it after Bill told her what happened. I know that prick Harrington. I know where he likes to drink when he's off duty. When you're ready, let me know. I'll

take you there. Buy you a beer." Sammy smiled. "Or something."

The implication was clear. Rodney Harrington was in for some hurting.

"Say, what's the matter? Why're you holding your arm like that?"

"Busted," Longarm said. "Rodney and his magic nightstick."

"Bill said he thought the bastard hurt you. He didn't say nothing about it being broken, though. We get back to the house, the doctor can look at you. He's a good sawbones. Knows what he's doing. He takes care of all the girls."

That did not seem like such a wonderful reputation as far as Longarm was concerned, but if the man was good at what he did, so what? Longarm had been treated by a horse doctor before and lived to tell about it. So why not a man who specialized in social diseases?

"Look, I'm a little shaky right now. Could we get a cab back to the house?" Longarm asked.

Sammy smiled again. "Got one waiting outside. Come along now before Constable Harrington sees us leaving and arrests the both of us out of pure meanness. The bastard."

The doctor surprised Longarm. He was a young man with dark hair and a pencil-thin mustache. He had a pointed little patch of chin whiskers and a dark red birthmark on the left side of his neck.

He looked at Longarm's arm, which had swollen to half again its usual size and taken on the shape and coloration of a dead trout. It also hurt like a son of a bitch when Dr. Stamp examined it.

"When did this happen?" he asked.

"This morning about dawn," Longarm told him.

Stamp grunted, picked up the arm and looked at it again. Then, very gently, he laid it down. "You probably know that with a break like this one, conventional wisdom has it that you should immobilize the broken member and allow the swelling to subside before you attempt to set and tightly wrap it. Unfortunately that all too often allows the bone ends to begin the healing process when they are not properly aligned. That could seriously affect your use of the arm. Not only while it completes the healing but permanently."

"I sure don't want that," Longarm told him.

"Of course you do not. So I want to set it now, before the bone ends start to knit themselves back together. If I do that, it will hurt like hell. I'll give you some laudanum to quell the pain." The young man smiled. "Enough of that and you won't care if I cut the arm off. Which I do not like to do even when it is a medical necessity. This, luckily, is a simple fracture. I will set and splint it now. The splint will have to be re-wrapped every day or so until the swelling has completely subsided. Then," he shrugged, "you wait. In a month or so, depending on your overall state of health, the arm should be as good as new." He paused and smiled again. "I hope."

"Doctor . . ."

"Stanley. Call me Stan. Everyone does. When you say 'doctor' like that, it makes me feel old."

"I don't care how old you are, Stan. I sure as hell care how good you are."

"Oh, I'm very good, Mr. Long. I am *very* good. Now drink a slug of this laudanum. That's good. Now another. Fine. Go ahead. Finish that little bottle. I have more."

The pain that had been wracking Longarm's entire body began to grow fuzzy around the edges, and his thoughts drifted lazily on moving clouds.

He could see what Stan was doing. Now Stan and Sammy and Bill too. Holding him. Pulling back on his shoulder and away on his wrist.

That should have hurt, but there was only a twinge of pain. Then the world swirled and danced merrily away in a kaleidoscope of bright, gleaming colors.

Chapter 21

Longarm woke up with a dull ache in his right arm and a light-headed wooziness like he was coming off a ten-day drunk. It took him a few moments to remember just why his arm was in a splint. Once he did, it began to hurt worse, throbbing in time with his heartbeat.

His mouth was dry and he felt sure that his bladder was about to bust from containing so much piss. When he tried to sit up on the side of the bed, he had to make four attempts at it before he managed, and even then his head swirled bad enough to make him sick to his stomach.

He did better when it came to standing upright. He managed that after only two tries. The victory was short-lived. When he tried to take a step toward the thunder mug that sat under the tiny stand where the water pitcher and wash-basin were stored, he lost his balance and went crashing onto the floor.

"Shit!"

He landed heavily on his side, mercifully on his left side. The jarring from the fall made the broken arm hurt bad enough, without his whole weight coming down on that shoulder too. Longarm rolled slowly onto his belly and tried

to push himself upright. He was on his third attempt when the room door opened.

Honey came in, her face a mask of worry. "Are you all right?"

"Yeah, I just . . . gotta get up, that's all."

"What you need is to get back in that bed, mister," the girl ordered.

"Look, I got to, um . . ."

"You have to pee?"

"Yeah. Like a horse. I feel like my belly is about to bust open."

"Let me get you back on the bed. Then I'll bring a jar for you to pee in. No, never mind that. You can use the water pitcher. I can wash it out afterward."

While she spoke, the pretty black girl was already in the process of helping lift Longarm more or less upright and steering him onto the bed.

"But . . ."

"Don't you 'but' me. I already seen you bare-ass naked. Nothing you got is going to surprise me. Now hush up and lie back."

She emptied the heavy crockery water pitcher with the colorful pictures of flowers decorating it, pouring the contents into the washbasin. "Here now."

The girl pushed the leg of his drawers aside and pulled out his pecker, guiding it into the mouth of the pitcher.

"Open your legs a little. Go on. Do it. I ain't going to rape you."

Longarm did as she said. He felt the cool rim of the pitcher. Felt the warmth of her hands. Then gratefully he opened the floodgates and let his piss flow.

When he was done—he would have sworn he could piss more than that pitcher would hold, but in fact he only half

filled it—Honey set the pitcher aside, pulled a cloth from her apron pocket and very gently wiped his cock and cleaned it off.

"Thanks," he told her. "I can't b'lieve I had t' go that bad."

"Of course you would," Honey returned. "You've been sleeping in here for almost three days."

"Three . . . Shee-it!"

"Oh, it's true. The doctor has been to see you twice. He said to just let you sleep, that it was good for you."

"No wonder I'm so hungry then. An' thirsty. Could you . . . ?"

She smiled. "Of course I can." Then she laughed. "Just don't drink out of that pitcher before I get back." She turned and hurried out into the hallway. He could hear her steps receding toward the stairs.

Longarm closed his eyes and tried to ignore the constant, gnawing pain in his arm.

"Honey?" He sat up. He was alone in the room, but it was obvious that Honey had been back already.

A small folding table had been brought in and placed beside his bed. It held a pitcher of water—different pitcher, fresh water—a cup already filled with water and a plate of assorted cookies and candies. Not his usual fare, but any port in a storm. Longarm gratefully drank from the cup and nibbled on one of the cookies. Almond-flavored, he thought, and very sweet.

He finished the first cup of water and two more just like it before he slowed down.

He did not know how long he had been sleeping this time, but his head was clear now. And he had to piss again.

Longarm stood—just a little wobbly when he did so—and took the two steps to the washstand. He pulled the

thunder mug out from the shelf under it and relieved himself into it.

Then, weak but much improved, he went back to his bed and again sat on the side of it.

He was tempted to sleep again but he had things to . . . Come to think of it, he didn't have shit to do right now. He was not yet ready to resume his duties as Sammy's helper. Soon, perhaps, but not yet. So when you got right down to it, there was no damned reason why he should not take another wee nap.

Longarm lay down again, bunched the thin pillow under his neck and closed his eyes.

Chapter 22

"What are you . . . ?"

"Shh. Hush now." Honey's voice was gentle and comforting. It was sometime during the night, for his room was dark save for one stubby candle burning on the side table and a little light that seeped in from the hallway by way of the transom. "Hush, baby."

Longarm almost laughed when she said that. Baby? He was probably half again her age.

Laughter would have been horribly insulting, though, considering what the girl was doing.

She had already unbuttoned his balbriggans and was busy trying to work them off without waking him. That part had not worked, but the reason she was doing all this certainly aroused his interest.

Aroused more than merely interested, in fact. Aroused his pecker to rigid attention also, because in between tugging here and there at the cloth, she was stroking here. And there.

Longarm shifted on the bed enough to help her get the light cotton balbriggans off him, and Honey immediately began to fondle his already hard cock and his balls.

"Oh, I see you're plenty awake now," she said with a laugh.

"Don't complain t' me about what you found there, missy. It's your fault that it's happened."

"Then perhaps I should do something about it."

Honey stood and quickly stripped off the pale shift she was wearing. She stood there naked in the candlelight.

"Turn," Longarm said softly. "Nice an' slow, turn around so's I can see you from all sides."

"You don't think I'm ugly? A nigger girl that works in a whorehouse?"

"Don't you call yourself that, Honey," Longarm snapped. "Don't you *ever*! You are a lovely young woman who's deserving of respect."

"You don't think . . . ?"

He smiled. "I think you're beautiful." "Beautiful" was stretching things maybe. But she was pretty enough. And very sweet.

"You wouldn't be ashamed to be with me? In bed, I mean. You wouldn't mind to fuck me?"

"Honey, I would be pleased an' honored t' take you into my bed, an' for that matter, tomorrow afternoon I'd be proud to squire you right down Colfax Avenue where all the folks could see."

"I almost think you mean that, Mr. Long."

"I'm Longarm to my friends, Honey. An' I surely do mean it, every word. Now hush up your own self an' come here." He shifted over to the far side of the bed and opened his arms to her.

She came shyly to him. She smiled as she lay down and snuggled tight against him.

Her flesh was cool and soft. Her breasts when she lay on her back had little more bulk than a saucer turned upside-

down. Her nipples were like tiny black raisins, much darker than the creamy milk chocolate hue of her face and belly. Her pubic hair was like tightly wound coils of blue-black spring steel.

She was thin, almost painfully so, but she made up in warmth and caring what she may have lacked in bulk. She put her arms around Longarm and clung to him for a minute with her face pressed into the side of his neck. Then she pulled back just a little and whispered, "Can I kiss you?"

Longarm's answer was by deed instead of word. He kissed the pretty girl and she opened her mouth to him. He slid his tongue across her lips and over her teeth. After a moment, Honey responded in kind, her tongue probing into his mouth, hesitantly at first and then more boldly.

"Oh, I like this," she whispered.

Longarm chuckled. "That's why folks do it, Honey. It's why they do this too." His hand slid down across the softness of her belly and into the jungle of her hair. He found the opening to her pussy, already engorged and dripping wet.

A moment more and he felt the tiny bump that is the seat of a woman's pleasure. He toyed with it—very lightly—and Honey's breathing became quick and ragged. After not more than a minute or two her body stiffened and she cried out.

"I don't . . . What . . . Oh, God. Are you . . . What did you *do* just then?" The quivering in her voice suggested she was close to tears.

"Good Lord, girl. You really don't know?" He pulled his hand away from her crotch and held her body against his, stroking her back as if he were gentling a skittish colt. And perhaps he was. "You don't know what that was?"

She shook her head.

"That, dear, is what all the working girls pretend t' have when they shout in their john's ears."

"I never felt anything like that before," Honey confessed.

"Listen, you aren't a virgin or anything like that, are you? I mean, there's some as set high value on stayin' a virgin. I wouldn't want t' take anything away from you an' the gentleman you someday marry."

"I'm not a virgin," she assured him.

Longarm grinned. "Then lay back an' open your legs, Honey. You got something down there that I want t' explore with more than just a fingertip."

"Do you want me to French you first?" she offered.

"You know how t' do that?"

"Oh, yes. Christina . . . You don't know her, she hasn't worked here in a long time . . . She taught me how." She giggled. "She made me practice on a cucumber. But you're bigger than it was. I know how, though. Really."

She moved down the bed until she was kneeling between his legs, then dipped her head to him. Her mouth was warm and encompassing. That said, she did not know how to suck cock worth a damn. She failed to grasp the part about "suck" and just held her mouth loosely over the head of his pecker.

Not that there was anything wrong with that. Exactly. But it fell far short of satisfying.

"That was nice. Now let me do something here," Longarm said. He pulled her up beside him and pressed her down flat on her back.

"You won't hurt me, will you? You're awful big."

"I'll go slow an' give you time t' adjust," he promised.

He did, but even so she cried out when he was only a

few inches in. After that one yelp she was able to relax and lift her hips to his ever deepening thrusts.

Longarm took his time—there was no reason to hurry—and was rewarded when Honey climaxed again shortly before he hosed her belly with cum.

It was only afterward when she reluctantly drew away from him and stood, sweat-sheened and lovely in the candlelight, that she said, "You know what I told you? About not being a virgin?"

"Uh huh. I remember."

Honey giggled. "I lied." Then she grabbed up her shift and fled from the room.

Longarm lay back, smiling toward the ceiling. Hell, he'd already figured out that the girl had lied to him about that.

He did not regret what the two of them had done. It had been her choice.

Hell of a nice girl, Bill's daughter.

Longarm rolled over and closed his eyes.

Chapter 23

"Are you sure you're ready to go back to work?" Sammy's tone of voice was heavy with skepticism. "You just been back three days."

"Sure," Longarm told him. "Laying around makes me nervous. I ain't used to it. An' this busted wing is gonna hurt no matter what, whether I'm sitting on my butt upstairs or down."

"If you're sure."

"Just ask Miz Cleo for me, will you?"

"I already did," Sammy told him.

"So what'd she say?"

"She said you can sit on your butt."

"What?"

Sammy grinned. "She said we're to pull this little table around and put it beside the stairs. She wants you to set behind it and look stern."

"Stern, eh?"

"That's what the lady said. Said it won't hurt to remind the gents that we aren't gonna take any crap from them. They can be beat up and tossed out just like any other bum if they get too far out of line."

"I didn't know that was possible," Longarm said.

Sammy grinned again. "It depends on how much money they're willing to pay for their fun."

"Just how much do they pay anyway?"

Sammy rolled his eyes. "Plenty. It can run into the hundreds if they want to take a girl permanent."

"Permanent? D'you mean buy a girl like for a slave or something?"

"Oh, I suppose they could do that too. But there are," he hesitated, "there are other reasons."

"I don't understand what you mean, Sammy."

"Look, you're one of us. Miz Cleo trusts you, and you'll find out what I mean one of these days. But why borrow trouble if you don't have to? It's the sort of thing a fella might be happier not knowing."

"All right. If you say so. Miz Cleo trusts me an' I trust you, so I reckon we're okay here." Longarm pushed his chair back and got up from the kitchen table.

He picked up his revolver and stuck it behind his belt. The damn thing poked him hard in the belly when he sat with it still in place, and he did not yet have the use of his right hand, so he could not wear the gunbelt Sammy had found for him.

"Oh, that's another thing," Sammy said. "Miz Cleo saw the way you like to lay your pistol on the table when you set. She liked the idea of that for when you're setting out in the hall too. Any commotion upstairs I can probably handle by myself, but if I need you I'll call out. Otherwise your job is to stay there beside the stairs with your pistol on display to sort of remind the gentlemen to act like, well, gentlemen."

"Unless they pay for the privilege of being wild," Longarm added.

"Yeah. Exactly. Come on now. Help me check the liquor supplies and the cigars."

"It's nice to see you up and around." He must have heard that sentiment or something very close to it a dozen times while the household prepared itself to receive guests.

"Good t' be up an' about, believe me," he responded with heartfelt sincerity. Longarm had the patience of Job when it came to lying in ambush for game—or a felon—but none at all when it came to lying around with no more purpose than to heal. Taking time to heal pissed him off.

He was healing, however. Bill and Honey came in each day to loosen the wrappings on his splint and tighten them down snug again to account for the reduced swelling. Another day or two and he expected the arm to be back to its original size and—more important as far as he was concerned—its original shape as well. That fishbelly shape and color immediately after the break had *not* looked good.

Good food and clean living accounted for his quickness to heal, Longarm figured. Those things plus fine cigars and rye whiskey. He helped himself to plenty of those while he sat around knitting his bones together.

Now, back to work more or less, he felt pretty good again.

He had little enough to do. He sat there wearing a shirt that had one arm snipped away so he could get it on properly and an overlarge suit coat to cover the splint. It was entirely possible that the gents passing in front of him would not even know he was injured. Better if they did not actually.

He also was careful to keep the black slouch hat on, with the brim drooping low over his eyes.

With his beard closely trimmed and neck shaved—the

whiskers itched when he tried to grow them out on his neck—he looked unlike the tall, dapper deputy United States marshal who used to ride for Billy Vail.

Longarm was content to leave it like that.

He settled in behind his table and waited. It was not yet dark when the bellpull jangled to announce the first guest of the evening. Time to get to work.

Chapter 24

Over the next few days Longarm discovered that he knew, or at least recognized, most of the gents who patronized Miss Cleo's house of great comfort. He had seen them in the better class saloons, theaters and dining rooms of the city, where he too once spent his leisure hours. It was an advantage—if advantage it was—he had not expected.

If any of them recognized him, they made no comment. Not to his face anyway. Longarm had no quarrel with that. He had no desire to be recognized here as a former deputy U.S. marshal, now disgraced and cashiered.

This job was not exactly on a par with that one.

On the other hand it was not entirely bad either. He had all the cigars and pussy he wanted. Probably could have had all the excellent rye whiskey he could handle too, but he was going light on that nowadays.

And the work was not exactly onerous. He sat on his ass behind a table with his hat brim pulled low and glowered at the customers, reminding them that not quite anything goes.

There were moments of excitement now and then, however.

His fourth night behind the table he heard a raucous

commotion in the parlor, where masculine voices were shouting and whistling. Much more, he figured, and someone outside the house was sure to call the Denver police. No one wanted that intrusion.

Longarm stood and used his left hand to push the barrel of his Colt behind his belt, then walked the few steps to the wide double doors leading into the ornate parlor.

He grunted when he saw what was going on. It was no wonder the gents—there must have been upward of a dozen of them in the room enjoying their cigars and whiskey—were whooping it up. They were encouraging two of the girls in an impromptu performance of sorts.

Tall, lean and elegant Frederica, who was as black as a sculpture carved out of anthracite, was licking Helene, a pudgy blonde who was so pale she looked artificial. The girls seemed to be enjoying themselves. Certainly their audience was.

Longarm was well aware by that point that most of the working girls, as they preferred to call themselves, got nothing out of the constant grunts and groans and ejaculations of their clients. Some had boyfriends. Some had toys. And some turned to other girls for a sad semblance of love. It appeared that Helene and Frederica fell into that category.

Not that Longarm was going to condemn them. Whores have feelings too. Or so he had been told.

Still, he figured it was his job to protect the house, and this amount of noise could not be allowed to continue. Longarm stepped inside the parlor.

"Gentlemen. Listen to me." No one did, and the noise continued unabated.

"*Dammit!*" Longarm barked in a booming parade-ground voice.

The noisy merrymaking slacked off, even if it did not completely cease.

"Girls," Longarm snapped. "Helene. Frederica. Stop what you're doing there."

The two whores stepped back away from each other, and the room became instantly silent.

"I don't want t' take anyone's fun away," Longarm said in a softer voice, "but we don't want any trouble with the police. We don't. I'm sure you don't neither. So let's be quiet about this." He smiled and said, "Uh, girls, you can go back to what you was doing if you like."

Frederica leaned down and gave Helene a deep, passionate kiss. The smaller girl put her pale hands on Frederica's ebony tits and caressed her lover.

The gents loved it. But they were quieter in their enthusiasm this time.

Longarm turned to go and found himself nose-to-nose with Miss Cleo.

"I, uh, hope you don't mind," he said. "I thought it needed doin'."

"You did the right thing, Long. You did just what I was coming to do. Thank you."

"Yes, ma'am."

Miss Cleo headed down the hall toward the office where she conducted her business with the gentlemen callers, and Longarm went back to his table.

Five minutes later he had reason to regret making that appearance in the parlor.

One of the gents emerged from there, Sheila on his arm and a half smile on his face. Sheila hung half a step back when they stopped in front of the table. She gave Longarm a wink. He suspected that meant she would be by to see him after working hours ended.

It was the gent who interested him though. The fellow was short, slightly built and graying at the temples. He was clerk of the municipal court in Denver. He would have been the man who signed the orders that sent Longarm to jail on charges that many a man would have walked away from with no more than a judicial slap on the wrist. Canfield, Longarm thought his name was.

"I know who you are," he said as if accusing Longarm of something. Of being who he was perhaps.

"Yes, sir?"

"You're that murderer Long. It was in the papers about you. You shot down a peace officer, shot him in cold blood. Got away with it too. You wouldn't do that in my court."

"It was an accident," Longarm said, thinking that it was not Canfield's damn court.

"Don't you argue with me," the man snapped. "Don't you dare."

"Yes, sir." Snapped? Longarm could have snapped this scrawny little popinjay in two and he wouldn't have needed his busted right arm to do it. "As you say, sir."

Canfield paused long enough to glare at Longarm another moment or so, then he led Sheila up the stairs.

Longarm felt sorry for her. She was a nice girl. Janie in real life. Canfield was not likely to treat her as a person who deserved some consideration, some happiness.

Still, Janie could handle the little bastard. And if she could not, well, Longarm would be pleased enough to help Sammy bust the little prick up just a little.

He sighed. That much was just fantasy of course. The gents were never hurt. Not unless Miss Cleo herself gave the order.

Longarm returned his attention to his sit-and-do-nothing job.

Chapter 25

Sheila escorted Leonard Canfield to the door about an hour later. The little prick looked entirely satisfied with himself. Longarm was sorry to see that.

Normal procedure was that Sheila should now go straightaway to a washroom off the kitchen and get the soap, water and vinegar needed to clean herself and prepare for the next gentleman. Miss Cleo demanded that the girls do that immediately. She did not want a guest to see a girl who had not yet douched and perhaps insist on going upstairs with her. Delay was not permitted.

Even so, Sheila came instead to the table where Longarm was sitting.

"I need to talk to you," she whispered.

"Something Canfield said?"

The girl nodded.

"Can it wait till after work?"

"Yes, I suppose so. Can we, um, get together then?" she asked, making it obvious that she had more than the verbal form of intercourse in mind.

"You know where I'll be," he told her.

Sheila glanced down the hallway behind Longarm. He

suspected she was worried lest Miss Cleo see her lollygagging there when she was supposed to be in the washroom preparing herself to receive another gentleman.

"Later then," he said. "Go on now."

Sheila hurried away, and Longarm went back to his duties, such as they were.

He sat on the side of his bed, naked but for a towel laid over his lap. He would not have bothered with that except he was smoking one of Miss Cleo's fine cigars, and he did not want to risk having hot ash fall into his lap. That was *not* a pleasant prospect.

The expected tapping came shortly after the coach lamps that flanked the front door were extinguished, signifying that the house was closed for the night.

Longarm stood and opened his room door for the caller. He blinked and stammered out a brief hello.

Honey did not appear to notice his hesitation. She came to him and hugged him tight. "I've missed you so much," she whispered. It had been probably forty-eight hours since they were together.

"Are you all right? Is anything wrong?" he asked.

"Everything is fine. I just . . . I just miss you so much when I'm not with you. I know I'm just a silly nigger girl, and you are a fine gentleman. The real thing, not like the men who come here. But I think . . . I think I love you. Do you mind? I don't expect you to love me back. But I hope you won't mind if I love you, Mr. Long."

He kissed her and stroked her hair. "There ain't any more compliment that a girl could give to a man than that, Honey. Thank you."

"You don't mind then? You really don't?"

"I really don't," he assured her.

"Will you make love to me? Please?" She was already taking her clothes off. "There is something I would like to do," she said as she stripped away the last bit of fabric and stood before him naked and no longer shy.

"All right."

"Lie down, please. Go ahead."

He did so, stretching out and bunching a pillow under his neck.

Honey plumped the pillow for him, then tugged his knees apart. "Now close your eyes," she said.

"I, uh . . ."

"I won't do anything to hurt you. I promise."

"I never thought you would."

"Then close them. Please."

He did. He felt the bed shift as Honey crawled onto it with him. Then he felt her hands lightly caress his balls and his cock. If he had needed any encouragement to begin with, that touch provided more than enough. His pecker stood to attention and began to throb.

She cupped his balls in her hands. And then he felt . . . warmth. Moisture. A sweet, steady pull.

Longarm smiled. "You been taking lessons from some o' the girls, haven't you?"

He felt her nod, his cock still in her mouth at the time. A moment later the warmth was replaced by a light, cooling chill as she withdrew and allowed the air to reach his wet dick.

"Rosemary is the best cocksucker in the house," Honey said. She clearly intended the term as a compliment, not a condemnation. "She has been teaching me." She giggled. "We got a cucumber from the kitchen for me to practice on. The first one wasn't big enough so I got a bigger one. Rosemary wanted to know who I expected to be with, but I

wouldn't tell her. She would just want to take you away from me. Rosemary likes big dicks."

"I'm glad you didn't tell her," Longarm said, mostly to make Honey feel better.

"Let me show you. I can take it all. I think I can anyway."

"Can I open my eyes now? There's nothing prettier to a man than a pretty girl with his dick in her mouth."

"If you like that, sure." She was smiling up at him when he opened his eyes, her skin dark against the pale red of his engorged cock. Her eyes seemed huge, her lashes very long.

"Show me," he said.

She licked and fondled him for a little while first and got him good and wet. Then she took a deep breath and with another sweet smile lowered her face onto him.

He could feel the ring of cartilage at the back of her mouth. Honey hesitated there for a moment, and he could feel her begin to gag. Then she overcame the impulse and pushed down on him again, hard, and the head of his cock slid fully into her throat.

Minutes later they were still like that, Longarm flat on his back and Honey kneeling over him with her throat full of hard cock, when there was a sharp, metallic click.

The bedroom door swung open.

Janie gasped at the sight of Longarm lying there with the house help.

Then she charged forward.

Chapter 26

Janie grabbed a handful of Honey's hair and yanked. Hard. Honey flew backward, instantly pulled off Longarm's cock. She yelped. Or Janie did. He really could not be sure who was making the more noise, Honey with her startled cries or Janie with her cursing.

"Black bitch! In here messing with my man."

"Let go of me. You're hurting me."

"He was mine first, nigger."

"Leave me be."

"I'd beat you black and blue except you're already black."

"That hurts. Let go!"

Janie clung to Honey's hair, dragging her backward around the small room, Honey on her butt bouncing along behind the furious white girl.

"But I didn't do anything," Honey was protesting.

"You bitch. You're trying to steal my boyfriend."

"My hair. You're pulling it clean out."

"I'll pull all of it out of your cheating head, I will."

Honey managed to turn so that she was duckwalking in a squat, arms flailing to the sides, hair still firmly in Janie's

grasp. Janie had wrapped a thick hank of Honey's hair around her hand and had no intention of letting go.

Thoroughly enraged by the way she was being mistreated, Honey decided to fight back. She balled her fist and punched Janie square on the pussy. Janie shrieked and began pummeling Honey's back with her free hand.

Honey managed to get her feet under her and drove upward, head-butting Janie in the belly. Once she got to her feet, she began punching Janie in the tits.

"Damn you, you motherfucking bitch."

"Whore!"

"Nigger!"

"Cunt!"

Longarm figured it was time to pull them apart. He stood and—very carefully—took hold of Janie's wrist with one hand and Honey's with the other.

"Let go of her hair now, Janie. It's all right. You can let go now. Honey, quit your punching. You've done enough for one night. Okay? Good. Now settle down, both of you. Janie, I want you t' set on the bed. That's right. Right there. An' Honey, you move over there. See that stool? Set on it." He shook his head. He could not claim that it was in disbelief, however. Longarm had learned long ago that he could believe pretty much any damn thing of a woman, especially an excited female.

Still naked, he sat on the end of his bed so that he was positioned between the two. They could not easily get after each other that way, he figured. But if he had to, he could grab his Colt and whack one of them over the head with the barrel.

"Now then," he said. "Janie, as you could plainly see, me an' Honey was, um, busy when you came in. She was showing me how good she'd learned stuff."

"She learned some of it from *me*," Janie wailed. She began bawling, tears running down her cheeks and snot running out of her nose.

"Did not! Rosemary taught me," Honey shot back. "Everybody in the house knows you don't suck cock worth a damn."

"Why, you black bitch, I'll—"

"Hush!" Longarm barked. "Both of you settle yourselves down. Right now. You hear me? Right now."

"I'll be quiet. Fine. But you and me are through. We're quits, mister. I wouldn't let you near my pussy again if you paid Miz Cleo for me, and I *sure* wouldn't never suck that dick of yours again neither." With that, Janie got up and flounced out of the room, leaving the door standing open with a good many of the working girls crowded out in the hallway looking to see what all the commotion was about.

"All right, ladies," Longarm said. "The show's over. You can all get back t' your beds now."

He closed the door in their faces and turned to Honey with a rueful smile and a shrug. "Sorry 'bout that, girl."

"I . . . Would you mind if I didn't finish what I started? Not that way, anyway."

"I understand," he said. "Come here. Lay down an' let me hold you."

The girl was trembling. It took quite a while for her to calm down. And for Longarm's hard-on to return.

Somewhere along in there he remembered that Janie had wanted to talk to him about something. Something she saw or heard or learned when she was with that asshole Leonard Canfield.

He hoped it was not something important because it was damn sure doubtful that Janie would be confiding in him any longer.

Chapter 27

Longarm tapped lightly on the door. He heard a voicc from within invite, “Come.” He turned the knob and entered the boss’s office. Miss Cleo was seated behind her desk.

“You wanted t’ see me?”

The woman nodded. “I have been hearing things about you, Long,” she said.

He felt a flutter of worried anticipation. She must have heard about that wrestling match between Janie and Honey a few days earlier. Likely if anyone was going to be fired, it would not be one of them. And in truth he had been the cause of their dissension. He had to admit that.

“Sammy tells me you have been doing a fine job. He likes you. So do the girls. They say you protect them but don’t stare at their tits. They like that.”

“Yes, ma’am?”

“I must admit that I had my doubts about you when you first came here, you being a former deputy marshal and all. But you have worked out very well.”

“Thank you, ma’am.”

“I intend on giving you more responsibility in the future, Long. I feel I can let Sammy have a few days off.”

"That's very kind of you, ma'am." Longarm felt a sense of considerable relief. He had thought he was about to be cashiered. Again.

"What am I paying you, Long?"

He grinned. "Damn if I know. I ain't seen any of it yet."

"Really?" She looked surprised. And perhaps embarrassed as well. Quickly she pulled her cash box out of a bottom drawer and extracted some coins. Bright, shiny, *yellow* coins. Those were the very best kind. "Here."

Longarm extended his hand and Miss Cleo dropped two double eagles and a ten-dollar piece into it.

"Thank you, ma'am," he said again. "Would it be all right if I leave the house an' go spend some o' this?"

"Aren't you being well served here?"

"Yes'm, completely, but I want t' go see about getting some new clothes. These work well enough t' keep me from walkin' around naked and scarin' the gentlemen, but I'd like to see can I find something that fits a little better."

"I wouldn't mind at all, Mr. Long. You can come and go by the back door. It is never locked."

"Thank you, ma'am. Thank you very much." Longarm took his pay and left the office.

"What in the world are you doing looking at those off-the-shelf goods, Longarm?"

Longarm turned and greeted the clothier who had met his needs for the past several years. "H'lo, Tim. I've come a peg or two down in life. Maybe you haven't heard. Point is, it's true. Now I need something cheap an' sturdy. Three shirts, I think. Something with a big enough sleeve that it will go over this here splint. Two pair o' britches. Half dozen pair o' socks. An' this vest, I think." He picked up a

leather vest and tried it on. The fit was a little loose in the belly, but he had a small waist for his chest size so that was to be expected.

"An' boots," he said. "Lordy, I do need some decent boots that don't have t' be laced for half a damn hour to get them on in the morning. Can you give me all of that?"

"Of course. Shall I put those things on a tab for you?"

"No, I'll pay cash. I tell you what, Tim. I got some errands to run. How about I go tend to that stuff, then come back t' pick up my purchases?"

"You don't want to choose your colors and styles?"

"Hell, Tim, I trust you t' pick what's best. Would you do that for me?"

"Of course."

Longarm was not surprised. He had given the shopkeeper a good deal of business over the years. "I won't be long," he said.

The telegraph operator gave Longarm a skeptical look, then glanced down again to reread the message form in his hand. "Sir, you know, don't you, that this address is only six or seven blocks distant. It would be cheaper and quicker for you to drop it off there yourself."

"Thanks, but I'm in a hurry. Don't have time t' go over there and anyway my handwriting is terrible with my arm like this. You'll type it up proper an' deliver it for me, won't you?"

"Do you have cash to pay for the service? I will have to charge you as if it is a regular telegraphic message."

"I have cash. How much will it be?" Longarm smiled disarmingly and reached into his pocket for the smallest of the coins Miss Cleo had given him.

• • •

"Wrap those up, Tim."

"Don't you even want to look them over first?"

"Not at all. You know my sizes better'n I do anyhow. I know you've picked out good stuff."

"All right then. Let me tie them up in a tidy bundle so you can carry them easily. You said you want to pay cash?"

Longarm usually placed an order, took delivery of his things and eventually got around to paying what he owed. The management of money was not something he normally gave much thought to. "I do," he said this time. "How much do I owe you?"

"I already have your bill written up. Everything included, it comes to, um, eighteen dollars and eighty-five cents."

Longarm handed him one of the $20 double eagles and said, "Put the change against what I owe you from before, please."

Tim smiled. From Custis Long that was entirely unexpected.

As soon as Tim finished wrapping and tying it all, Longarm tucked the bundle under his right arm, adjusted the position of the Colt that was stuffed into his waistband and ambled out the door.

He was whistling a merry tune as he made his way back to Miss Cleo's house of delights.

Chapter 28

"Queen of England."

Longarm could faintly hear the girl's shout for help somewhere on the third floor. He was in the second-floor hallway. He dashed up the staircase and burst onto the third-floor landing.

"Queen of England."

Two doors down, he thought. On the right.

Longarm tried the doorknob. Locked. He moved a step backward and kicked the door solidly just to the side of the latch. The door popped open and he stepped inside, a little cautiously, if the truth be told, since he had no idea who or what was in there.

He saw tiny Immaculata in her baby girl mode, hair in twin braids and a rag doll clutched to her chest, cowering in the corner at the head of her bed. She was naked and bloody, although Longarm could not see where the blood came from.

Standing over her, also naked and covered with dark hair, was a man Longarm had often seen around the courthouse. The john held a wicked lock-blade folding knife that he waved at Immaculata. She in turn pressed herself

deep into the corner and kicked at the hand holding the knife.

Longarm assumed the john had already cut her, probably many times judging by the amount of blood that was flowing.

It was Longarm's job to put a halt to the unauthorized abuse—if the fellow had paid for the privilege of chopping up the little girl, Longarm would have been tipped off—and ideally to do so without damaging the customer. Had it been left to Longarm's discretion, he would have stopped this the easy way: by putting a .45 slug through the son of a bitch's temple. Messy but damned well effective.

As it was . .

"Please put the knife down, sir."

"Go fuck yourself. This little cunt needs a lesson in manners. I'm jus'," he paused to swallow, "just the man to give it to her."

"I'm sure Miss Cleo will be glad to impose any discipline that is required, sir. Just inform her of the problem. She will take care of it. In the meantime I'd like you t' please put that knife away. Then I'll personally take you downstairs t' see Miss Cleo about this." He faked a smile. "How's that sound, sir?"

"Go fuck yourself. You aren't taking my knife away from me."

"No, sir. I only asked you to fold it up and put it away."

"I could cut your dick off, you know. An' I jus' might too." The john turned toward Longarm and waved the knife back and forth. Longarm figured that was an improvement. At least he was not threatening Immaculata with it now.

"Mr. Hightower, I'm askin' you nice. Put the knife away."

"Or what? What are you gonna do if I don't? You can't touch me. I know how it is around here."

"Yes, sir, and I will get my ass in deep shit if I feel it's necessary t' shoot you. But you know who I am. You know I'd do it. One bullet and I could put you in a pine box. Or I could drop in the courthouse t' see how my case is progressing. I know some fellas there as might be interested in how the assistant prosecutor spends his time. They might like t' know how you can afford a place like this on the money the city pays you."

"You son of a *bitch*!" The last word came out as a barely intelligible shriek and the man lunged at Longarm.

Longarm's Colt flashed into his hand. He slammed the barrel and cylinder hard against Adrian Hightower's temple. Right where a bullet should rightly go, although this would simply have to do.

Hightower's eyes rolled back in his head and he dropped to the floor at Longarm's feet.

Longarm looked at little Immaculata, who had not yet ventured out of her corner. "It's all right now, Mac. He's not gonna hurt you anymore. How bad are you cut?"

"I will heal." She began to cry. "He wanted to kill me. He thought it would be fun. I thank the God above that he did not pay Miss Cleo enough so he could do that."

Longarm blinked. Even the possibility of such a thing turned his stomach.

"Can you do something for me, Mac?"

"Anything, Mr. Long. The rest of my life belongs to you. Anything you want, I will do."

"What I'd like for you t' do, Mac, is t' put something on, then go downstairs an' tell Miz Cleo what's happened. Then go back to the kitchen an' get Bill t' stanch those cuts an' put some salve on them. Can you do that for me, please?"

"Anything, Mr. Long. I mean that. Anything."

He smiled at her. Maybe . . . when she was feeling better . . .

"Go on now. Tell Miz Cleo, then find Bill."

The girl scampered off the bed, grabbed up her robe and hurried out into the hallway.

Longarm picked up Hightower's knife and admired it for a moment. It was nicely made and probably very expensive. He took it to the doorway and wedged the blade between the door and the frame. One good push and the blade snapped off. Then he perched on the edge of the rumpled bed and waited for the gentleman to come around.

Chapter 29

"How did it go while I was away?" Sammy asked when he returned from taking a few days off.

"Nothing I couldn't handle," Longarm told him.

Sammy poured coffee for both of them and glanced toward Bill, who was standing at the stove. Sammy leaned forward and lowered his voice a little. "I heard there was some trouble with that asshole Hightower."

"Like I said. Nothing I couldn't handle."

"The problem with him," Sammy said, "is that he's a big part of Miz Cleo's umbrella."

"Um . . . oh. You mean he gives her cover," Longarm said.

"Him and some of the others who come here."

"Do they get to ride free?"

"No, of course not."

"Reduced price then?"

Sammy shook his head. "No, her protectors pay full price for their pleasures. They ought to. The sons of bitches have plenty to spend."

"They aren't actually living on their pay from the city or the county then," Longarm said.

Sammy snorted. "Not damn likely." He took a small sip of the hot coffee and smacked his lips loudly, then turned and said, "Bill, you make the best coffee in this miserable city."

"Why, thank you, Mr. Sammy."

Longarm tried his coffee. Sammy was right. It was damn good.

"Custis, could you do me a big favor?"

Longarm was tired from working all night but, hell, he was low man on the totem pole here. Whatever needed to be done, he was the one who would do it. "Glad to, Miz Cleo," he said.

"I need this liquor order delivered. You needn't stay to collect any of it. They will deliver. But we need some of these items before the gentlemen arrive this evening, so please tell them to send my purchases immediately."

"Yes, ma'am. What if they tell me they can't get to it right away?"

The fat woman smiled. "They will not do that, believe me."

"Yes, ma'am." He took the envelope from her hand.

"You do know where, don't you?"

"Yes, ma'am. I was there with Bill a couple times before."

"Good. Hurry on then. You will want some sleep after such a long night."

Longarm grabbed his hat and headed out the back door. Honey was on the porch, cutting pieces of the sea sponge that the girls inserted into themselves to keep from becoming pregnant. The sponge worked fairly well but had to be replaced often.

"Were you looking for me?" She sounded hopeful.

"Sorry, darlin'. Miz Cleo gave me an errand that needs doin'. How's about tomorrow morning?"

Honey smiled. "I'll come up as soon as I can then."

He looked around to make sure none of the others were watching, then bent down and gave her a brief kiss. Her lips were soft and moist with promise. "Tomorrow," he said.

Actually this errand he was on now should not take all day, but . . . no, tomorrow would be better. He had to get some sleep.

Longarm hurried down to the creek and followed it to the next footbridge, then crossed over with his boots dry. Once on the other side he hailed a hansom and headed first—and very briefly—to the liquor wholesaler's to drop off Miss Cleo's envelope, then back by way of a Western Union office.

He dismounted from the cab within an hour and a half of leaving, paid the driver and started back across the narrow footbridge.

He was halfway across when he noticed someone standing on the other end, feet planted like he was ready to fight.

The sound of boot heels striking wood came from behind. Longarm turned his head to see. That end of the bridge was blocked too.

The man standing in front of him wore two pistols and a fancy silk waistcoat. He probably thought himself quite a dude. The one behind had only one revolver, but there was something about the way he carried himself that suggested to Longarm that this one knew what he was doing.

Mr. Two-Guns would be the easier to take, Longarm judged. Mr. Rough-and-Ready might be a handful. And that was the one who was at his back.

The only question now was whether they wanted to beat him up and rob him or if they were waiting here to kill him.

When in doubt: Ask.

"What'll it be, boys? I don't have enough money on me to make robbery worth your while."

Two-Guns answered. "We ain't here to rob you, Long. There's people that don't like you."

Longarm smiled. "That's fair 'cause I don't like your ugly ass. Now get outa my way or suffer the consequences."

Predictably, Two-Guns chose the consequences. He grabbed for his right-hand gun.

Chapter 30

Longarm was not sure just what they'd expected. Perhaps they'd thought he would stand there, petrified with fear of being braced by the two of them. Or frozen in terror at the sight of Two-Guns' menacing scowl. The man was obviously emboldened by the fact that Longarm's broken right arm kept him from being able to use his right hand effectively.

And possibly they thought he would burst out laughing at the sight of Two-Guns trying to drag his Colt out of the leather.

Longarm did none of those things.

The man standing behind him was the dangerous one. Longarm knew he had to take care of that one first.

He dropped onto the planks of the narrow bridge, twisting as he did so. He ended up flat on his back.

While he was falling, he yanked the single-action Colt .45 out of his waistband and cocked it. By the time he hit the wood, he had the Colt leveled at the dark, dangerous thug who had been behind him.

That one already had his revolver out and was trying to take aim, a process made more difficult by the twin facts

that his target had just dropped below his line of sight and his partner was now standing *in* his intended line of fire.

Longarm had no such problem.

He squeezed the trigger and felt the .45 buck in his hand.

For a moment his vision was obscured by the plume of white smoke that belched from the muzzle of the Colt.

Behind him Two-Guns screamed, "Johnny!" The idiot was wasting time worrying about his pal. Good.

The smoke blew away. Good buddy Johnny was on his knees and going down, a .45 slug in his chest.

Longarm rolled quickly, belly down, left hand extended, Colt aimed now at Two-Guns, who by then had managed to haul one of his pistols free but who was peering beyond Longarm toward his dying friend.

Longarm was not in a mood for sentiment. These boys had been sent to kill him.

He took careful aim and fired, hitting Two-Guns in the right elbow. The man screamed again, this time in pain, and dropped his right-hand gun. If he remembered that he even had a left-hand gun remaining, it did not occur to him to go for it.

"You've shot me, damn you."

"So I have," Longarm said, rising cautiously to his knees with a backward look at Johnny, who by now was down, his blood spilling off the edge of the little bridge and into the creek below.

Longarm was almost positive that Johnny was already dead. Almost. Which was not good enough for someone who would again be behind him.

He raised his Colt, took careful and deliberate aim, and shot Johnny in the top of the head. Gray brain matter squirted

out of the man's ears and his extremities drummed briefly on the planks.

Two-Guns screamed, his face twisted so that Longarm thought he was going to cry. "You didn't have to *do* that!"

"Maybe, but it's the safe thing t' do."

Longarm crossed the bridge to Two-Guns, who was on his knees, left hand clutching his shattered right elbow. The man likely would never have proper use of that arm again. Certainly he would not be able to learn the fine art of the quick draw, not with his right hand.

Longarm stood looking at him for a moment, Two-Guns staring fearfully up at him. Then Longarm used the side of his boot to sweep Two-Guns' dropped revolver—it was a Remington, a handsome weapon with inlays on the grips and engraving on the steel—off the bridge and into the water below. He reached down and pulled a matching Remington from Two-Guns' left-hand holster. The injured bullyboy did not object. Longarm tossed it into the creek also.

"What are . . . what are you gonna do to me?"

"Ask you some shit. Kill you if I don't like your answers." While he spoke, Longarm flicked open the loading gate of the Peacemaker and shucked the empty cartridge cases out. Each landed on the bridge with a bright *ping*. Two-Guns stared at them. And at Longarm when he reached into a pocket and brought out some cartridges. He took his time about reloading the revolver.

"Now," he said. "Let's you an' me have that talk, eh?"

"But I'm bleeding. Won't you at least wrap my arm to stop the bleeding?"

"Nah, there's no point in that. Not if I'm gonna kill you anyway." He smiled. "An' that's a question we can work out between us right here an' now."

Two-Guns looked like he might faint. He was pale and probably going into shock.

"Back up," Longarm said. "Off the bridge. I don't want you t' topple over an' fall in the water. It's all right if you drown, but not before you tell me what I wanta know. That's fine. Right there will do. No, stay on your knees. It's a position that looks real good for you. Now . . . about that conversation you an' me are fixing t' have . . ."

Chapter 31

Longarm smiled, the expression twisted and evil. He palmed his Colt and held it to the wounded man's nose, using the front sight to hook the fellow's left nostril so that Longarm could lift the man's head by that means.

"That hurts."

Longarm pulled the revolver back half an inch, moved it lower and pushed it forward again, the muzzle this time sliding into the fellow's mouth. There was a moment of resistance as he bumped up against the man's front teeth. Longarm pushed again, harder, and the muzzle slipped free.

"There! Isn't that nice?" He held the .45 in place there, then pulled it out and carefully wiped spit off the muzzle. The man turned his head and tried to spit but could not. Apparently his mouth was dry. Not that Longarm could figure out why.

"Taste bad, does it?"

"Bitter. It tastes like steel. I expected that. And oil. But . . . it tastes awful bitter too." There was more than a hint of whine in the fellow's voice when he said that.

"Know what that is?" Longarm asked conversationally.

"It's residue from the burnt gunpowder. You know. From when I shot your friend there."

"I . . . He wasn't . . ."

"Oh, hell, of course he was." Longarm smiled again, walked over to the footbridge and perched on the side, leaning back against one of the wooden uprights that carried the handrail above. "Dead now, I think. Though I could shoot him again t' make sure. What d'you think?"

"Oh, Jesus. Don't ask me stuff like that."

"Tell you what. Let me ask you something easier. What's your name?"

"Maury. Uh, Maurice. Maurice Albert Showalter."

Longarm smiled again. It was not likely that the expression would be seen as reassuring. "And your dead friend back there was Johnny what?"

"John Taylor. That's what he said it was anyway."

"Thank you." Longarm idly brought the hammer of his Colt back to half cock and rolled the cylinder around. The rolling mechanism made a soft, well-oiled sound. If he looked—and Longarm was confident that he would—Showalter would be able to see the dull gray lead of unfired bullets in the rotating cylinder.

"So, Maury, I got a big one for you this time. Who hired you t' jump me an' blow my lights out?"

"I . . . I don't know. I swear to God, mister, I don't know who it was. Me and Johnny was in a bar . . . I don't remember which one . . . and a fella approached us. He said there was a lot of money in it if we was to take down this dude name of Long. He . . . he described you pretty good."

"Even what I was wearing?" Longarm asked.

Maury nodded his head vigorously. But then the man was pretty well worked up by now. Longarm was fairly cer-

tain Maury would admit to killing the pope and all three wise men if the question were put to him properly.

"He gave us fifty dollars and told us what to look for," Maury volunteered.

"Fifty dollars each?"

Maury shook his head no. "Fifty between us. But he said we could keep whatever you had on you."

"Where's the fifty now?"

Maury nodded toward his dead friend. "Johnny's got it. In his right-hand pocket, I think."

"You realize, I hope, that if I don't find fifty dollars there to corroborate your story, I'll figure you were lying an' shoot you."

"Oh, Jeez. Oh, Jeez!" A dark stain began spreading across the front of Maury's lap. The simpleminded son of a bitch was peeing himself. "I ain't lying to you, mister. I swear I ain't."

Longarm's smile was positively evil. "We'll see, won't we? Now tell me more about this fella you say hired you two idiots t' undertake a grown man's job."

It was a good twenty minutes later before Longarm finally stood, his joints creaking, and walked back across the little bridge. He stepped carefully over Johnny's body, bent down and retrieved fifty dollars in crisp new currency from the dead man's pocket.

Then he turned his back on Maury and walked over to the Western Union office before finally heading back to Miz Cleo's house of many pleasures.

Chapter 32

Longarm yawned. It had been a long night. Much more tolerable now that he was back to full duties—not that they were burdensome to begin with—but even so, they were long, slow and for the most part boring.

He went downstairs, where Bill and Honey were busy cleaning the parlor. Sammy was in the kitchen bent over a cup of coffee.

"Hello, Custis. Can I pour a cup for you?"

"Thanks, but my belly's sour already. Been drinking coffee all night tryin' to stay awake. Now that I can head for the bed, coffee's about the last thing I'd want. What I came down for is t' see if there's anything you want me to do before I turn in."

Sammy shook his head. "No, I can't think of anything that needs to be done right now. We can handle the restocking this evening, after Bill has the place cleaned and ready."

"That suits me. In that case, Sammy, I'm gonna go help myself to a shot o' rye to settle my stomach, then see if I can crawl up them stairs one more time."

"All right. I'll wake you about five," Sammy said.

Longarm touched the floppy brim of his slouch hat in silent salute and ambled back into the parlor.

Bill was busy pumping one of the newfangled vacuum cleaners. The pumping action somehow created a vacuum which, in theory, was supposed to suck up any dust or tiny bits of litter off the carpet. As far as Longarm could see, a plain old broom and dustpan worked better. But then what did he know about cleaning carpets?

Honey was coming along behind her father, dusting the furniture and arranging things in proper order. When Longarm took up a glass and poured himself a shot of rye, the girl laid her feather duster down and came to stand close beside him. She glanced toward her father to see that he was not paying attention, then whispered, "I need to see you."

"All right," Longarm said, his voice low.

"In your room? Soon as I'm done here?"

He nodded, tossed down the shot and looked at Bill, who by now was watching them. "I'll take the glass upstairs with me," he said in a normal tone, then picked up the decanter—he needed to refill it later, he noticed—and headed for the staircase.

When he got to his room, he was as tired as if he had been breaking rocks all night long. He set the glass of rye down and kicked off his boots, shoved the Colt beneath his pillow and stripped down to his balbriggans. Honey had seen him in his smallclothes often enough before now. And in considerably less than that. There was no point in worrying about it now, he figured.

He had been waiting perhaps a half hour when he heard the light tapping on his door.

"Come."

Honey slipped inside, small and slim and pretty. Long-

arm stood to greet her, and she rushed into his arms, lifting her face for the expected kiss. She was breathing rapidly.

"Whoa," he said. "What's the rush? You said you needed t' see me. What's wrong? What's this about?"

"I just . . . I've missed you so awful much, Custis. You haven't had me for days and days. Don't you like me anymore?"

Shit, if he had known that was all this was about he would have told her some flowery crap and put her off for a day or two, until he could catch up on his rest.

Too late now, of course. By the time he thought about that, Honey already had half her clothes off and was tugging at what little remained.

Longarm took a moment to step out of his balbriggans so that he too was naked. Then again he took the girl into his arms, her ebony flesh in lovely contrast with his pale skin.

She felt good against him, warm and small and soft.

He kissed her, probing her eager mouth with his tongue, then drawing back and guiding her onto his bed.

"Oh, I've missed you so much," she whispered.

"Me too." He was not sure he meant that, but it was a nice thing to say.

"You're such a beautiful man. Here. Roll over on your back and lay still now. Let me enjoy myself."

Longarm did as she asked even though he was more than half afraid that he would fall asleep in the middle of her pleasure.

Uh, no. There was less danger of that than he'd thought. When the tip of Honey's tongue touched his left nipple and began making slow, wet circles around it, all thoughts of sleep fled. Instantly.

And his erection was about half a heartbeat behind that.

It sprang up like a tent pole and began gently bouncing up and down with each fresh pulse of blood.

Honey cupped his balls in the palm of one small, warm hand while she bathed his chest with her tongue, paying particular attention to his nipples, moving from one to another and back again. It was something that he knew she especially liked to feel herself.

After several minutes of that, she licked and nibbled her way down across his belly. He was prepared to feel her take him into her mouth, but she bypassed his cock when she got to his crotch and pushed his legs apart so she could lick his balls and suck on them.

While she did that, she ran a fingertip lightly around and around his tightly puckered asshole. When he was rather thoroughly worked up, she slipped the tip of that finger inside him.

"Uh, I . . . That ain't my favorite thing," he said.

She immediately withdrew it and went back to what she had been doing.

Only when his balls had been thoroughly licked did she lift her head enough to capture the head of his throbbing cock. She licked it too, but only briefly. Then she took his cock into the wet heat of her mouth and began to suck.

Longarm felt sure he must have died and gone to heaven. Honey, who had been a virgin only a few weeks earlier, was a natural as a cocksucker.

He lay back and let the girl have her way with him.

Chapter 33

Longarm reached down and ran his fingertips gently over Honey's cheek, enjoying the hollowed feel due to the suction she was applying to him.

He ran a finger alongside his cock, sliding it up inside her mouth so that he could feel the hard, rippled roof of her mouth and the wet pressure of her tongue on both his dick and his finger at the same time.

He felt inside her cheek and along her teeth, then withdrew his finger and laid it, wet with her saliva, on the outside of her cheek again.

"Damn, but you are one pretty li'l gal."

Honey mumbled something that he could not understand but knew would be positive.

He cupped her face in the palm of his hand and gently pried her away from his cock. She made a moist, plopping sound when the head of his dick came free.

Honey looked concerned. "Is something wrong?"

Longarm smiled down at her and shook his head. "Not in a hunnerd years. Not while you're doing that."

"Then why . . . ?"

"I wanta look at you. I like looking at you, pretty girl."

Dark as she was, he thought for a moment she flushed even darker as she blushed at the compliment. "You mean that?"

"That an' a helluva lot more. Come up here now, please. I wanta kiss you."

The girl scrambled up his body and flung herself smiling onto his chest. Her mouth on his was soft and wet, and her breath was sweet.

He could feel his hard-on bouncing lightly against Honey's round little butt.

"Lift up a minute there," he said. "That's right. A little higher." He reached down between them and took hold of his cock, held it to the dripping wet opening to her pussy and said, "Now down. There. There. Oh, yes."

Honey smiled as she felt him slide inside her body.

"Are you comfortable?"

She nodded vigorously.

"Now sit up. That's it. Kinda spread your knees an' sit on my thighs. Ah, that's nice. It feels good." He smiled at her. "An' I can look at you at the same time."

Lordy, she was one pretty little thing. Slender and young and sleek, her skin with the satin perfection of youth and health.

Her small tits were a rich chocolate brown color. The nipples that sat at their tips were as black as coal and almost as hard. Longarm reached up and fondled her tits. He rolled her nipples between his fingertips, and Honey's eyes glazed and her mouth sagged just a little as she gave herself over to the pleasures Longarm taught her.

"Sweet," he whispered. "You're awful sweet."

He felt of her soft, flat little belly and ran the ball of his thumb lightly over the little bright red nub of her clitoris.

Honey began to shiver with the intensity of a climax.

She ground herself hard against him and cried out, then collapsed, limp and utterly spent on top of him.

"Is there someone . . . Ay yi, I am sorry."

Longarm looked up. Immaculata was standing in the open doorway. The little Mexican whore glanced behind her, into the hall, then stepped the rest of the way into Longarm's room.

"I am sorry to . . . you know. Sorry." She looked embarrassed, then a sort of professionalism took over and she came forward and stood beside the bed peering closely at Honey.

"You know, girl, you have a cute shape. You could make good money with that figure."

Longarm was pretty sure that Honey blushed, but again he could not be positive.

"What is it, Mac? What's brought you to my room?"

The girl returned her attention to her original purpose. "There are people, Mr. Custis. They would kill you."

It was Honey, not Longarm, who cried out in protest.

"Get off for a minute, Honey," Longarm said. "I gotta talk with Mac. We, uh, we'll finish later on. I promise."

Chapter 34

All three perched on the edge of Longarm's bed. Honey wrapped a sheet around herself. Longarm just sat there. He figured Immaculata was not likely to be offended by the sight of a naked male. If she even noticed, she gave no sign of it.

Honey, Longarm was amused to see, tucked herself close beside Longarm and hooked her arm through his elbow, staking her claim here. He thought it kind of cute of her.

"Now, Mac. What's this about people wantin' t' kill me?"

"Señor Custis, I would be dead now if it wa'nt for you." Shc leaned forward to look at Honey. "Did he tell you what he done? He save my life, that's what he done."

Honey squeezed Longarm's elbow but kept her mouth shut. The pretty Negro girl was probably well versed when it came to remaining quiet among her betters.

"I tol' you, Señor Custis. I would do anything for you."

"An' I appreciate that, Mac, but what . . . ?"

"This evening. Tonight. I am playing the baby schoolgirl for a gentleman. He likes the young ones, you know?

So I pretend I am virgin." She laughed. "I am a good virgin. I do this many times. The gentlemen, they know better but they preten'. An' I am small for them. Down here, I mean. My alum does this for me. The gentlemen, they like to have a virgin. Especial a virgin that can do the things I do for them, eh?"

"Okay, but . . ."

"I am getting to that. Let me explain."

Longarm closed his mouth and vowed to keep it that way. For the time being.

"Okay, so I am with this gentleman, yes? An' next thing you know, the door opens. Like now. With you. The gentleman an' me, we are doing it. I am crying. He is *rojo* . . . red in face. Here. And here." Immaculata demonstrated with her hands, indicating her cheeks and neck.

"He is about to finish. Then he see we are not alone an' he loses it." She made a sound like a teakettle running out of steam. "He slide out of me and says nasty things I would not ever say," she crossed herself, "and sit up all red in face again but for different reason now.

"Well," she said, "Sheila is there in my room. *My* room. She has never been in my room before this time, never. We are not so good friends, no? Now she is there. She motions for my gentleman to come, but when she look out into the hall, she shuts the door again and sits on the side of the bed. *My* bed. Like we do here now. You unnerstand?"

Longarm nodded. Honey acted like she had not heard.

"Sheila takes the han' of my gentleman an' she tells him that the plan did not go good. She say she gave the money to someone. He give it to someone else. These someone try to get Custis Long out of the way, but Señor Long kill them both an' rob them of the money."

Honey squealed. "They tried to kill Custis?"

"*Sí*," Immaculata said, bobbing her head emphatically. "She say they try to do this thing. Is this so, Señor Custis?"

Longarm grunted. He did not actually admit to anything, though.

He was thinking about the report that he killed two would-be assassins. That was mighty interesting, considering the fact that Maury was very much alive when Longarm left him on that bridge.

Either someone was lying about Maury . . . or someone killed the wounded man after Longarm left. To keep him from pointing fingers, perhaps?

"Sheila tol' my gentleman that she would need more money so she could get someone better than them to take care of Señor Custis. Then she lean forward again so she can look at me with a mean, evil face and she say that she will get me if I say anything about what I hear. I tell her I will not tell. But that was a big fat lie. Mr. Custis save my life. I don' tell her that."

She sighed. "I wait until Sheila goes to bed for the night. Then I sneak upstairs to fin' you an' warn you."

"Thank you, Mac. You're a mighty good girl, an' I appreciate you."

She beamed like he had just given her a most wonderful present.

"Now tell me about this gentleman of yours," he said. "The one Sheila talked to. And did they say anything about *why* they were going to all this trouble?"

Immaculata shook her head. "No, señor. But you know what I think. I think you should not trus' Sheila no more. I think if that man gives her more money, she keep it. Try to kill you her own self."

"That's probably good advice, Mac. Now tell me about the man, please. Did he give you a name? What does he

look like? How tall? How does he dress? Docs he carry a gun? Tell me everything you can remember, please."

All of a sudden Longarm was not nearly as tired as he'd thought he was. If anything, he was wide awake and would have trouble getting to sleep today.

Chapter 35

There were probably a hundred men in the city of Denver who would fit the description that Immaculata gave of her "gentleman who liked little girls." Longarm knew only one of them.

He was surprised, though. Charles Rinker was one of the judges on the municipal bench. He had the reputation of being hard on crime. When at work, he was stern and unforgiving. When he was at play . . . Mac had a less charitable view of him. But she had experienced his play; Longarm had not.

"I need t' run some errands today," he told the girls. "Mac, you slip on outa here before you're spotted. Honey, check an' see the hall is clear, will you? Thanks. An', Mac. I owe you. I don't forget my friends."

He waited until Mac had gone, then took Honey into his arms. He kissed her and sighed. "Looks like we'll hafta finish what we was doing later. Will that be all right with you?"

"Anything you want is all right with me," she whispered. She snuggled tight against Longarm's chest for a moment, then released her hold on him and gathered up

her shift. She paused only long enough to step into her slippers and give him one more quick kiss, then Honey too was gone.

Longarm sighed again. He was tired, dammit. But this was not something he wanted to put off. He got dressed, shoved the Colt revolver into his waistband where he could get to it left-handed, then draped the misshapen black slouch hat on his head and slipped quietly down the stairs.

Miss Cleo and Bill were in the kitchen making up some sort of list.

"I thought you said you were going right to sleep," Miss Cleo said.

"Yes, ma'am, an' I tried. Couldn't seem t' get comfortable so I thought I'd take a little walk. That sometimes eases both the body an' the mind, you know."

"If you want to go out so badly, you can help Bill fetch these things in. We'll be having a special party Wednesday night. Invitation only, and we want things to be especially nice."

"Yes, ma'am, I'll be glad t' help."

Longarm sat and had a cup of coffee while he waited for the two to finish putting their list together. It would, he gathered, be some fancy soiree. They were ordering kegs of lobster, crab legs and oysters packed in ice, three dozen Kansas City steaks, tongues, oxtails, champagne, artichokes and half a dozen other items.

"Come along then," Bill said when the lists were done. He led Longarm out the back door and into the city.

"Are we carrying any of this stuff back with us today?" Longarm asked.

"Just the artichokes, and then only if I like the looks of what they got on hand. Miz Cleo, she does a world of business with these folk. They'll get in fresher and better if the

stock on hand ain't up to snuff. That's why I didn't ask for you to come along to begin with."

"Then would you mind if I go off and run an errand o' my own?" Longarm asked.

"Makes no never-mind to me. You go ahead and do whatever it is you got to do. You can catch up with me later."

Longarm grinned. "If you're still in town when I get done with my business. I, uh, have what you might call a friend. Her husband is off workin' during the day, don't you see?"

Bill laughed. "Lordy, I'd'a thought you'd got enough of that back at Miz Cleo's. But you're young. You still got the sap of a young bull in you."

"You don't mind?"

"Go on with you. Kiss that white girl on the pussy one time for me when you get her drawers off."

"Bill! I am shocked. Shocked, I tell you." But Longarm was grinning when he said it.

Longarm veered off to the side. He pushed through the batwing doors of a seedy, sour-smelling saloon and stood there watching until Bill was out of sight, then he hurried out onto the street again and turned toward a Western Union substation.

Chapter 36

Longarm caught up with Bill at the wine wholesaler's. "Hope I didn't take too long."

"Naw, you're fine. I told Miz Cleo there wasn't nothing needed doing today that I couldn't do myself."

"I appreciate having that time to myself, though. I want you t' know that," Longarm said.

The Negro cook nodded. "Believe me, I know something about being able to go and do as a man please." He did not comment further than that, but given Bill's age, there was a strong possibility, a likelihood even, that he had been born and spent considerable time as some white man's chattel property. He would indeed appreciate the small, simple freedoms that most people take for granted every day.

"What else do we need t' do now?"

"I already got thc seafood order in and the vegetables. Now we place the meat order, and we be done."

"That sounds good to me." Longarm yawned.

Bill laughed. "That's one of the few bad things about working in a whorehouse. When you gonna get some sleep?"

Longarm could not help but wonder if Bill knew that Longarm was fucking his daughter. Probably not, he concluded, or the man would not be so friendly.

When the shopping was complete, they headed back toward Miss Cleo's.

Longarm paused on a street corner to bite the twist off a cigar and light it, then asked, "Mind if I ask you something?"

"You can ask anything. What I tell you . . . that depends on what it is you ask."

"It's this private party Wednesday night. What's that all about? If you don't mind me asking, that is."

"Oh, I don't mind the question. Can't give you much of an answer, though. Me, I don't keep up with all this political shit. Far as I can figure, politics is all just a bunch of rich men trying to work out ways to get theyselves richer."

"Ayuh, that just about pegs it," Longarm said. "This party is for a bunch of politicians then?"

"Depends on what you call a bunch. Not so many expected Wednesday. Eight gentlemen, I think. Now you'll be wondering about the extry food. At a party like this the ladies participate too." Bill laughed. "There's even one gentleman who brings his wife along. Miz Cleo has to have a girl for her too, you understand. Everybody eats. Everybody has a nice time. Then the gentlemen close the door for a little while. When they come out, the party starts up again and they have the rest of the night to do whatever it is that they want. No talk of money either. The gentlemen can do whatever they like. The girls know to go along."

"Who pays for all this?" Longarm asked. "It must be damned expensive."

Bill shrugged. "I don't know. Never bothered to think about that before."

"Do these parties happen often?"

"Not so very often. Maybe," Bill paused to think, "maybe three or four times before this one. Why?"

"Oh, nothing important. I was just wondering. You know. Because it must be so awful expensive."

"It sure be that. Miz Cleo takes in a pile of money every night, Custis. She has to be getting paid plenty to close up except for her private friends."

Longarm grunted. He walked on to the whorehouse with no further questions asked. He was thinking plenty, though.

Chapter 37

Longarm normally came awake quickly alert and aware of his surroundings. This time his exhausted sleep must have been barely minutes old. He did waken, but slowly, his mind dulled by the depth of the little sleep he had managed to get since returning to Miss Cleo's.

He was dimly aware that the door to his room had been opened. He could smell . . . what? A floral scent of some sort. He thought he should recognize it, remember it.

Or was he imagining this whole thing? He honestly could not decide. He was—

Shit!

A wraith was in his room. A ghost. A specter. It drifted in white, filmy clouds.

Closer. Closer.

Jesus!

Longarm threw his arm up, and Janie's knife blade thumped hard into the padded wooden strips that formed Longarm's splint.

The whore cursed in frustration and tried to wrench the knife away for another attempt at stabbing him.

Longarm twisted his arm, snapping the tip off the blade but freeing the knife for a slashing cut.

He pushed her away with his left hand, got enough separation between them to enable him to kick Janie in the stomach. She was launched backward toward the door, recovered her balance and came at him again.

Longarm was damn sure awake by then, adrenaline shooting through him like a charge of electricity.

"Hold it!" he snapped, reaching under his pillow.

For a moment Janie did halt in the middle of her assault.

"I don't wanta shoot you," Longarm warned, "but I will if I got to."

Janie's face twisted with hatred. "You're bluffing me, you bastard."

"I'm telling you—"

She lunged for him again, the knife upraised ready to slash him.

He had no choice, dammit.

He pulled the big Colt .45 from beneath his pillow and triggered a round point-blank into Janie's left tit. Her filmy nightgown caught fire, briefly flamed and then smoldered.

Janie stood tottering, still standing over him, still with the knife in her hand.

He supposed it meant he was no gentleman but . . . he shot her again. Carefully. Just above the bridge of her nose.

Janie's head snapped back and the light of life went out of her eyes. She toppled forward onto her knees and then to the floor, the knife falling with a clang onto the wooden boards.

Blood began to flood the area under her once-pretty head.

Longarm cursed a little, then stood, careful to avoid stepping in the whore's blood.

Chapter 38

"I don't know why she done it," Longarm told Miss Cleo, who had been helped up the stairs by Bill.

The little room was crowded to capacity and then some. Longarm, Miss Cleo, Bill, Sammy . . . and the dead girl. All were packed inside while a good many other wide-eyed, curious faces, including Honey's and Immaculata's, were gathered at the doorway peering in at the blood.

Tragedy is always popular, Longarm thought. As long as it is someone else's tragedy.

"How do I know it happened the way you say it did?" Miss Cleo demanded.

Longarm grunted. "You can see plain enough that the body hasn't been moved. You can tell that by the way the blood is pooled there an' there. See what I mean?"

"Maybe," the heavyset queen of the house conceded.

"An' there's her knife," Longarm added.

"I don't see any knife."

"Exactly. She dropped the knife when I shot her the second time. It'll be on the floor underneath the body."

"How do I know that?"

"'Cause in a minute I'm gonna show you. Besides

which, you can see here. Right here. You gotta look close, but that right there is the tip o' the knife she tried t' stick me with. I blocked the knife with my splint"—there seemed no point to mentioning that it had been a purely reflexive act that had him bring his arm up when he did—"an' the tip of it broke off in the splint. Right there."

"I still don't see any knife."

"I might need some help t' pick her up, seein' as I only have the one hand to work with."

"Bill," Miss Cleo said. The woman was still puffing and gulping for breath after the climb to the third floor. "Move the body, please."

"Oh, ma'am. Don't make me do that. Please."

"Hell, I'll do it," Sammy said. He wormed his way to the front, bent down and unceremoniously took a handful of Janie's hair, using it to jerk her torso off the floor.

Beneath the body the floor was free of blood. And the knife lay just where Longarm had said it would.

"See what I mean?" Longarm said. "Just like I told you."

"All right, but why would she attack you?"

Longarm shrugged. "Damn if I know." He did know. But that was not a subject he wanted to discuss with Miss Cleo.

"Look," he said, "now that you know I was telling the truth, I want t' know are we gonna call the police or not?"

The others in the room looked at him like he had gone suddenly daft. "No police," Miss Cleo said. "We do not call for the police here."

"But—"

"This is not something that hasn't happened before. This can be a rough business, after all. Things happen that we can't always control. But we always take care of them ourselves." She snorted, then turned to Sammy. "You know what to do."

"Yes, ma'am. I'll take care of it."

"All right now. Everyone go back to bed. We will be open for business again in a few hours, and you ladies need your rest."

The others slowly dispersed, Miss Cleo leaning on Bill's arm and the girls drifting off to their own rooms, until only Longarm, Sammy and the dead girl remained.

"What will you do with her?" Longarm asked, glancing down at the corpse.

"You don't want to know."

"Actually I do. It's clear this sort o' thing has happened before, so what d'you do with them when it does?"

"There's a fella has a farm a little ways east of town," Sammy said. "We take them there."

"You haul the bodies out to this farm to bury?"

Sammy gave Longarm an oh-grow-up look and said, "Bodies? What bodies?"

"But you said—"

"It's a *hog* farm, Custis. There ain't no bodies out there for anybody to find."

"Jesus!" Longarm said. It was bad enough that the girl had to die. Somehow it seemed worse to think of her being chopped up and fed to a pack of hogs. "Do you want me to, uh . . . ?"

Sammy shook his head. "No, thanks. I can take care of it."

Longarm shuddered, then he sat down on the side of the bed. All of a sudden he was bone weary. He lay back and closed his eyes. When he woke again, Janie's body was gone and Honey was there with a bucket and scrub brush.

Chapter 39

Longarm could not get the image out of his mind: Janie being eaten by a bunch of ravenous hogs. It was ugly. It would also be damned effective. No one would suspect. No evidence would be left behind. Lordy!

He sat up on the side of the bed and rubbed his eyes. "What time is it, Honey?"

"Time for you to stir, I'm afraid."

"Is Sammy back yet?" he asked.

"Yes, but he will take the night off. He wasn't able to sleep today, so you will have to watch out for the girls tonight."

Longarm nodded. By now he knew what to do.

He thought about taking a few minutes to pull Honey's drawers down and poke her. He was sure she would not object. But . . . not this evening. Not with that image of a dead, dismembered Janie still foremost in his mind. He stood and began to dress. It was time to get ready for the evening's work.

The night passed without serious incident. A few of the younger, more boisterous gentlemen thought about making trouble. Those thoughts did not last long. The last of them

left about four in the morning. Longarm locked the front door behind them and went to inform Miss Cleo that the house was empty. He found Sammy with her in her office, Miss Cleo seated at her desk and Sammy standing respectfully nearby.

"The last of them's gone, ma'am," Longarm reported.

"No problems?"

"No, ma'am."

"There is something I want you and Sammy to do before you go to bed," the fat madam said.

"All right, ma'am."

Miss Cleo looked up at Sammy. "Remember. One from the Chinaman and another from Rodney. I have already paid for them so don't let the Chink or Rodney try to talk you into anything extra. They will show you two or three to choose from. Pick whichever ones you think will work out best."

Sammy nodded. He turned toward the door and said, "Come along, Custis. Let's get this done so we can come home and get some sleep."

"Fine. What is it we're doing?" Longarm asked as they headed toward the back of the house.

"We need to pick up a couple more girls for the party tomorrow night."

"I'd've thought we had enough already."

"Nah, these are what you might call special girls. In case a certain special guest wants to . . . have fun with them."

"Sammy, I don't know what in hell you are talking about. Would you mind spelling it out for me?"

"I don't know as I should . . . Ah, shit, you're one of us now. All right. The deal is this. There is one gentleman in particular. Real powerful fella, he is. What pleases him is to strangle a girl while he is inside her. And of course Miss Cleo doesn't want anything like that to happen to one of

her regular girls. Not the good ones, anyway. So she buys what you might call disposable girls from other houses. She uses them just the one time, see."

"What if this fella doesn't, uh, like them?"

"She gives him a choice between two. He can pick between them. He knows he's not allowed to do that with any of the regular girls. Not without paying an awful lot extra anyway."

"And afterward they go to the hog farm?" Longarm asked.

"That's right. Nice and clean. No one knows anything about them. No one misses them. It's like they never was."

"This fella only uses one. What happens with the other one?"

Sammy shrugged. "Miss Cleo sells them on to some other house. These ones we're picking up tonight, they will be pretty enough. And young. The gentleman likes them young. But they won't have the parlor manners that sets Miss Cleo's house head and shoulders above the rest. All of our girls are good at more than just fucking, you know. Miss Cleo insists on that."

Sammy led the way to a sprawling, adobe maze with a wide veranda. The two of them waited on the veranda while the Chinese proprietor brought out three young Chinese girls. Each looked like she was in her early teens, but Longarm was no judge of an Oriental girl's age. To him they often looked far younger than they actually were.

Apparently none of them spoke English, but they seemed to know they were being sold. They stood, docile and silent. At their master's command they stripped off their clothes. Sammy looked them over carefully, had them turn several times and finally pointed at a girl with long hair and small, high breasts. "That one."

The Chinaman bowed and spoke to the girl, who stepped forward.

"Tell her to get dressed," Sammy said.

The other girls were dismissed, and the Chinaman spoke at some length with the girl he had just sold. She bowed to the Chinaman, then turned to Sammy and bowed again.

Sammy said, "I don't really need you to help me at Rodney's place so I want you to take this girl back to Miss Cleo's. Now don't look at me like that, Custis. She's just a damn Celestial. Take her on back to the house now before I get pissed off."

"An' do what about it?" Longarm said. But he grinned when he said it. He could hold his own against Sammy, and both of them knew it. He did not need to prove anything.

"Jeez, Custis. Go on now. Take this girl and go."

Longarm beckoned to the girl and turned away. She obediently followed behind him.

Chapter 40

The gentlemen began to gather shortly after night fell on Wednesday. Miss Cleo had had the household awake and scurrying for much of the afternoon. Everything and everyone was tidy and readied to perfection.

Every surface had been dusted, every rug cleaned. Brassware gleamed, reflecting the light of enough candles to stock a store. The tableware was polished, linen ironed and folded into clever representations of cocks and pussies.

Wine and whiskey were everywhere.

And the girls. They were extravagant confections of chiffon and silk and lace. Clouds of floral scent wafted on the air behind them. Longarm was more than a little amused by them. But then he had seen them hungover and exchanging farts at the breakfast table. He was not going to be fooled by the introduction of a little soap and perfume.

The gentlemen were admitted by special invitation only. All others had to be turned away with a smile and a hope they would return the next night.

By now Longarm knew virtually all of the gentlemen who patronized Miss Cleo's house. He just wished he knew which one among them was the "very special" guest who

would take his pick between the Chinese girl and the dark-haired, dark-skinned young Mexican, one of whom would be marked for sacrifice.

"I won't want you at your usual post tonight, Custis," he was told. "These gents won't need that sort of thing. But I do want you to wander in and out. As a reminder, so to speak."

"Yes, ma'am."

"And leave that revolver in your room. You won't be needing it."

"If you wish, ma'am." He hoped she was right about that, but right or wrong, the boss is always the boss.

"Go on now. Get rid of it. Then I'll have some last-minute things for you to do."

Instead of going up all three sets of stairs, though, Longarm went back to the kitchen, where Bill and two temporary helpers were sweating over the stoves.

"I wanta leave something in the pantry," he said. "I'll fetch it later."

Bill did not take time to speak. He merely nodded and went back to the careful, meticulous work of squeezing mashed potatoes out of a cake-decorating sleeve. A few minutes in a hot oven would turn the tops of the bite-sized puff pastries golden brown.

Longarm did not like doing it, but he had little choice. He slipped the Colt out of his waistband and debated the placement for a moment before stashing the .45 behind a flour box.

That done, he went back out to the parlor and checked yet again to see that every bottle was full and every glass sparkling.

This promised to be an interesting evening.

Chapter 41

Oh, it was fine. Bright lights. Sparkling conversation. The gentlemen and the ladies all dressed to the nines. It could not have been nicer.

From the back of the house one could hear the soft strains of a string quartet. Hungarians, apparently, with little English but exquisite musical ability.

Honey passed constantly among the guests, offering platters of this and glasses of that. French champagne was in great demand, as was Kentucky bourbon whiskey.

After forty-five minutes or an hour a handsome, white-haired man in white tie and tails arrived. Minutes later Leonard Canfield climbed onto a chair and banged a spoon against the side of an empty goblet to draw attention to himself.

"It is time, everyone. Time for you ladies to leave." He smiled. "But only for a little while. Go on now, please. Out. Out. Gentlemen, we will close the doors for a few minutes. When we are done, we will dine. Or . . . ," his smile was greasy, "whatever else you might wish."

The buzz of conversations intensified, then died away as Longarm and Sammy shepherded the whores out of the

parlor. Bill and Honey followed, and Bill carefully closed and latched the double doors leading into the hallway.

"Time to piss or repair your makeup or whatever else you need to do," he announced. "Find seats at the dining table so you'll be ready when the guests come out."

The girls trooped off toward the other side of the house. Bill stationed himself with his back against the doors, guarding the guests from any disturbance.

So much for Longarm's idea that he might slide over there under the transom and have a listen to what was going on inside.

Still . . . it was worth a try. He sidled over beside Bill. "Anything I can get you? Anything I can do for you?"

"You can move your white ass away from here," Bill hissed. "Does Miz Cleo see you here, the both of us are gonna be in bad trouble. G'wan now. Git!"

Reluctantly, Longarm went back toward the kitchen. He had not yet reached the entrance when Sammy stopped him. "I want you to go down in the cellar and bring those new girls up. Strip them naked first. Then bring them upstairs."

"What floor?"

"This floor. Take them to Miss Cleo's office. Keep them there."

Longarm walked past the pantry where his Colt was hidden and took the steep, narrow steps down into the basement. The cellar smelled of mold and moist earth. It was dark except for a shaft of light that came in through the open door above.

"Girls. Can you hear me? Time t' go up now." He had no idea if either of them could understand a word he said. Certainly the Chinese girl had no English. He was not so sure about the Mexican. "Come now, please."

Whether they knew the words or not, they got the message. Both of them appeared out of the darkness at the bottom of the steps. Both looked like they had been crying. He motioned for them to come, and they did.

Once up the stairs in the kitchen, Honey took charge of them. She hustled them out of their shifts, found a clean rag and dipped it in a basin so they could at least rinse their faces.

They looked very young and frightened.

"You take them on back there, Mr. Custis," Honey said. "I got to have the beverages ready when the gentlemen pull those doors open."

Longarm nodded. Again he motioned, and the girls followed.

As he led them down the hallway, Longarm believed he knew what a Judas goat must feel like when it leads lambs into the slaughterhouse. Or does the Judas goat not give a shit?

He knocked on Miss Cleo's closed door.

"Come," he heard from inside.

He turned the knob and pushed the door open.

Chapter 42

Longarm and the girls had not been waiting more than fifteen minutes when the door opened, and the distinguished-looking gent stepped inside with Miss Cleo close at his heels. When he saw Longarm, he stopped so suddenly that Miss Cleo ran into him, knocking him off balance for a moment.

"Long!" he snapped. "What are you about here?"

"It is all right, Your Honor," Miss Cleo quickly put in. "Custis works for me now."

Beyond her, Longarm could hear the clatter of footsteps on the staircase as the other guests took their girls and headed for the rooms upstairs.

"I don't like him being here," the gentleman complained. "You know what he is, don't you?"

"I know what he used to be. As I said, Your Honor, Custis works here now. He is a very good employee."

"I still don't—"

"He will be gone in a moment. Just choose the girl you want here, then he will take the other one away."

The judge looked a little put out, but he did as he was asked. He looked the two naked girls over from top to

bottom, motioned with his hand for them to turn around and inspected them all over again.

"I'll take that one," he said, pointing to the Chinese girl. "She looks like she has a lot of life in her." For some reason that comment caused him to laugh.

The old son of a bitch had a hard-on bulging the front of his trousers, and Longarm was sure the man was close to drooling in anticipation of what he intended to do to the girl's innocent flesh.

"You can take the other one back to the cellar, Custis."

"Yes, ma'am." Longarm cleared his throat as if to spit, pulled the window sash up and leaned out.

"*Come a'runnin'*," he roared.

If Billy Vail had gotten his messages all right and *if* everything went the way it was supposed to . . .

There was the pounding of axes on the front door and on the back. Men shouted and women screamed.

U.S. Marshal Billy Vail led the charge into the whorehouse. A stream of federal deputies and borrowed lawmen from nearby jurisdictions poured inside. Billy had not wanted to use Denver police or county deputies, because there was no way to tell which of them might have been involved in this scheme of justice for sale.

Before the first door could go down, His Honor Judge Calvin Holcomb was heading for the window.

Longarm grabbed for the man's arm, but without thinking about it he reached out with his right hand. The one that was wrapped in gauze to secure his splint in place. He tried again with his left hand, but by then it was too late. The judge scrambled out the window and onto the side porch.

They knew who the ringleader was now. There probably was no need to follow him. Billy could have the man picked up and taken in for booking at his leisure.

Still, Longarm's instinct was to chase his quarry. He dashed to the window and threw a leg outside.

Immediately he heard the crack of a small-caliber pistol shot. Likely something on the order of a .32 or one of the pipsqueak .38-calibers.

The bullet whined past, struck the side of the house and went singing off into the distance.

Longarm hesitated only for a moment, then ducked under the window sash and stepped out onto the porch.

The screams and foot pounding were all inside now. No one seemed to be left out back.

Longarm ran to the back edge of the porch and stood for a moment listening.

There! He could hear the crackle of breaking brush down by the creek.

If he had a damned gun now . . .

Longarm jumped off the porch, hit the ground rolling and bounced onto his feet again. He set off running toward the sounds down by the creek.

Chapter 43

The noise of precipitous flight stopped and the night became silent except for the burr of cicadas and the occasional distant call of a bird.

Longarm stopped. Listened for a moment, then crept forward again. He could hear . . . nothing. At least nothing of the Honorable Justice Calvin Holcomb. Behind him he could hear muffled screams and hoarse complaints at the "gentlemen" were rounded up and put in chains.

It was entirely possible that the only punishment any of them would ever receive was this one night of humiliation, so Longarm and Billy Vail planned to make the most of it. The arrested parties were handcuffed and chained together. When all were in control, they would be marched outside to waiting paddy wagons. By then reporters from all the area newspapers should be on hand to witness the little parade.

But Holcomb . . . there was no question that he would be charged. Including multiple counts of conspiracy. Murder too if Longarm had his way about it. And he thought he knew how he could.

In exchange for reduced charges and a lenient sentence,

Sammy would give up the hog farm to the east where bodies were disposed of. After that it would be a question of locating evidence.

Skulls are durable, Longarm thought, also the balls in hip sockets. Unless the hog farmer went to the trouble to burn the bones and break them up, there very likely would be physical evidence of the murders that took place in the whorehouse.

Miss Cleo and the judge should both go away for a number of years. Longarm hoped, however, that he could convince the special prosecutor to release the girls and the house help—Bill and Honey in particular—without charges. Longarm certainly owed Honey that much.

In the meantime . . .

He knelt and felt around on the ground until he located a stick. He tossed it toward the creek. The stick clattered into the brush.

There!

A footstep. And a wet, sucking sound. Mud. The son of a bitch was walking in the creek.

Longarm threw a second stick, this time aiming toward the sound he had just heard.

The noise spooked Holcomb. The judge cried out, probably startled by hearing something so close by. Longarm headed toward him. Carefully. After all, the judge had a pistol of some sort, while Longarm was unarmed.

Longarm picked up a rock and threw it. It splashed into the water, that sound immediately followed by the gurgle of someone walking in the edge of the creek.

"Give it up, Holcomb. Don't make me shoot you," Longarm bluffed.

There was a long moment of silence, then, "You wouldn't dare. Do you know who I am?"

"Yeah, I know. You're some asshole that likes t' hurt defenseless girls. Me, I'm a deputy United States marshal, you miserable turd, an' I'm taking you in on charges o' murder and involuntary servitude and I don't know what the fuck all else."

"You can't . . . You were cashiered. You are no deputy."

Longarm focused in on the sound of the man's voice, easing ever closer to Holcomb.

"It was a ruse, shit-for-brains, an' you fell for it. Now, are you gonna come out of there hard or easy?"

"I . . . My foot is stuck in the mud."

"Pull it out."

"These are my favorite pumps."

"Yeah an' they're garbage now. Now come outa there. *Do it!*"

"You don't have to shout," Holcomb whined.

"Out, I said."

Longarm heard some splashing, then saw the form of a man take shape in the darkness as Holcomb climbed out of the creek onto solid ground.

At some point in the past few minutes he must have tripped and fallen because now he was dripping wet, his clothes sodden and clinging to his tall frame.

"Hands up," Longarm ordered. "Give me that pistol." He could not actually see a pistol, but the asshole had one earlier. "Hold it up high. Higher."

"You are making a mistake, I tell you."

"Take it up with whatever special magistrate gets brought in t' hear this case," Longarm said. "An' don't think one o' your cronies will be sitting on the bench when you go before the bar. It'll be someone from another district. Now hand me that pistol."

Holcomb meekly surrendered a tiny Gambler's Ace

four-barrel pistol. No wonder he had not been able to hit anything. Longarm dropped the little gun into his pocket and took Holcomb by the elbow. "Come along, shit-for-brains."

They headed back toward Miss Cleo's house of great pleasure.

Chapter 44

"You son of a bitch!"

Longarm could not tell if Miss Cleo was snarling at him or at the Honorable Calvin Holcomb. Whichever, she was mad enough to spit. Her face was flushed dark red except for white rings around her eyes. The effect made her look like a raccoon, Longarm thought.

Indoors, in the glare of the many lamps and candles, Holcomb looked like a drowned rat. His hair was plastered tight to his head, and his breathing was ragged and fast. His complexion looked like that of someone who had already been through the embalming process.

Longarm displayed his catch with a certain degree of pride. After all, Denver justice had been for sale. That should come to an abrupt halt now, damn them.

And once these assholes were secured inside their cells, Custis Long fully intended to go looking for Police Constable Rodney Harrington and have a little discussion with the asshole about false charges and broken arms. Longarm flexed the fingers of his right hand. He was healing nicely now. Which Rodney would soon enough discover. The prick!

"Dutch," he said to another of Billy's federal deputies.

"Yeah, Longarm?"

"You got some handcuffs I can use on this water rat?"

"Right here, friend." Dutch dug into his coat pocket and brought out a set of government issue cuffs, which Longarm quite happily applied to an unresisting Calvin Holcomb.

"Let me know if those are too tight, Your Honor. We want you nice and comfortable when we toss you into a cell with a couple dozen of the poor sons of bitches you sent in there."

Holcomb declined to answer. But he did snarl something under his breath.

"Speak up, Your Honor. You're among friends here."

"Fuck you, Long."

Longarm laughed and gave the man a shove in the direction of the others.

Without warning, Holcomb's entire face and neck went suddenly pale. He gasped, his mouth gaping like a fish thrown on a creek bank.

The man stiffened, his head thrown back, and he fell facedown onto the floor. The sound of his nose and cheekbones breaking was ugly.

"Bastard's having a heart attack," Longarm said.

Ezra Jameson, the police lieutenant Longarm had supposedly killed by accident to start all this, was already kneeling beside the judge. Ez shook his head. "He is not having a heart attack. He had one. Past tense. That or something. Whatever the cause, he's dead."

Longarm grunted. He saw no reason to work up any regrets concerning the late Calvin Holcomb.

But he did need to get those handcuffs back so he could

return them to Dutch. He knelt beside the body and removed the bracelets.

When he looked up again, he was staring into the muzzle of a Colt .45.

Above the barrel he could see the cold fury in Miss Cleo's eyes. Off a pace or two to the side stood a very embarrassed young deputy. She must have snagged the revolver out of his holster.

There was not much question what she intended to do with the gun now that she had it.

Longarm spread his hands. "Easy now," he purred. "Jus' take it easy here."

"You destroyed a good thing here, you son of a bitch. I'm going to kill you for that. If it is the last thing I ever do, I am going to kill you."

Longarm realized it very probably *would* be the last thing the fat woman ever did. There were a dozen other lawmen in the room who would cut her down the instant that Colt fired.

It was a thought that gave Longarm scant comfort. As soon as Miss Cleo tripped that trigger, he would be a dead man.

Chapter 45

"Hold it! Just a second here. Hold it." Longarm threw his right hand up, fingers splayed as wide as he could get them with the linen bandage wrapped around his splint.

Miss Cleo's eyes automatically went to the white linen.

Longarm's left hand dipped into his pocket. It came out with the little Sharps hideout gun he had taken from Calvin Holcomb.

Before Miss Cleo had time to shift the focus of her attention, Longarm snapped off an unaimed shot.

He had no hope of hitting anything. Mostly he wanted to distract the fat woman with the burst of noise and smoke and flame.

It worked well enough. A thin spear of fire shot out of the Sharps, in the general direction of Miss Cleo.

Her mouth fell open, and Longarm assumed she wanted to shout, to curse, to say or do something that was important to her.

She had no time to complete the task.

Half a dozen revolvers exploded, filling the room with the stink of smoke from black gunpowder.

Half a dozen lead bullets slammed into the fat madam.

Bits of flesh and of blood flew; splattering those who stood nearby.

Miss Cleo dropped like a rag doll that had been tossed aside. The Colt she had been holding fell muzzle-down onto the rug. The jar of that impact was enough to dislodge the hammer sear, and the .45 fired. But into the floor, hitting no one.

"Shee-it!" Longarm muttered as he climbed—rather shakily he had to admit—to his feet again.

Both Billy Vail and Ezra Jameson rushed to his side. "Jesus, you did good," Ez said, thumping Longarm on the back while Billy grabbed his hand and pumped it.

"Hell, I had it easy," Longarm said with a grin. "You're the one as was dead for all this time."

Jameson threw his head back and roared with laughter.

Longarm looked at Billy Vail and said, "Boss, I gotta tell you. It's good t' be back."

"It's good to have you. And don't worry about a thing. I have your things, all of them. Henry . . . Where is Henry?" Vail looked around the crowded room. "Henry has your badge and identification. We were even able to get your old room back."

"Sounds good t' me, boss."

"One thing though."

"Yes, sir?"

"This is Wednesday. Tomorrow is a workday. I'll expect you in the office by eight thirty at the latest. You have a great many reports to fill out."

Longarm rolled his eyes, and Billy laughed. Jeez, it was good to be back among his own kind. "I would like t' ask you for a favor though, boss."

"Name it."

"It's about the Negro cook named Bill and his daughter, Honey. I want you t' let them walk away, boss. Please."

Billy hesitated only for a moment. Then he nodded. "If you say so."

"Thanks." Longarm yawned. "Now, if you don't mind, I intend t' sleep for two weeks straight. Your damn reports can wait."

"Like hell they can wait. Longarm. Deputy Long! Come back here. Don't you walk away from me like that. Henry, don't you dare give that man his badge back.

"Longarm . . . !"

Yeah, Longarm thought, it was good to be a deputy again.

Watch for

LONGARM AND THE PALO DURO MONSTER

the 363rd novel in the exciting LONGARM series from Jove

Coming in February!

GIANT-SIZED ADVENTURE FROM AVENGING ANGEL LONGARM.

BY TABOR EVANS

2006 Giant Edition:

LONGARM AND THE OUTLAW EMPRESS

2007 Giant Edition:

LONGARM AND THE GOLDEN EAGLE SHOOT-OUT

2008 Giant Edition:

LONGARM AND THE VALLEY OF SKULLS